LOW FLYING AIRCRAFT

L O W   F L Y I N G

Winner of

the Flannery O'Connor Award

for Short Fiction

A I R C R A F T

STORIES BY T. M. McNALLY

The University of Georgia Press

Athens and London

© 1991 by T. M. McNally
Published by the University of Georgia Press
Athens, Georgia 30602
All rights reserved

Designed by Erin Kirk
Set in Trump Mediaeval
The paper in this book meets the guidelines for
permanence and durability of the Committee on
Production Guidelines for Book Longevity of the
Council on Library Resources.

Printed in the United States of America

95 94 93 92 91   5 4 3 2 1

Library of Congress Cataloging in Publication Data

McNally, T. M.
    Low flying aircraft : stories / by T. M. McNally.
      p.   cm.
    ISBN 0-8203-1378-5 (alk. paper)
    I. Title.
PS3563.C38816L6   1991
   813'.54—dc20   91-14100
                                              CIP

British Library Cataloging in Publication Data available

Some of these stories first appeared in the following
publications: *Apalachee Quarterly*: "Ballistics";
Beloit Fiction Journal: "Peru"; *Hayden's Ferry Review*:
"Swans"; *New Times*: "Breathing Is Key"; *North Dakota
Quarterly*: "The McClenahan Stroke"; *Northwest Review*:
"In the Land of Milk and Honey and Jell-O"; *Other
Voices*: "Gun Law at Vermillion"; *Puerto Del Sol*:
"Paris, the Easy Way"; *Quarterly West*: "Jet Stream";
Wind: "The Anonymity of Flight."

The story "Gun Law at Vermillion" takes its title from,
and makes several references to, L. P. Holmes's novel
Gun Law at Vermillion (Lippincott, 1951).

The author would like to thank the Hotchkiss School
Summer Program for its support during the writing of this book.

The publication of this book is supported by a grant from
the National Endowment for the Arts, a federal agency.

FOR CHRISTINE

The dead will not lie still,

And things throw light on things,

And all the stones have wings.

Theodore Roethke

C O N T E N T S

LOW FLYING AIRCRAFT

PERU

Orion, 1986

When I first came back from Central America, I was thirty pounds light and still recovering from chronic dysentery. I'd gone south for a sanctuary group based in Tucson, a group of Catholics and some sincere but muddled graduate students. They had wanted me to "document the situation, do some good." I returned with a hundred and sixty spent rolls and a distaste for the political climate. Thirteen months down there will do that to you.

I flew to O'Hare on a United red-eye from L.A.X. The plane was wide-bodied and on it I leafed through a copy of a magazine I'd picked up in the terminal while looking for a bathroom. Following a spread on a women's volleyball team was a series of mine on the Contras: lots of stark shots of boys toting auto-

I

matic rifles and grenade launchers, a guy named Julio whom I later found dead on the bank of the Coco River with a bloodied rock near his head. They didn't have that picture. The magazine said I was a young and famous photographer; I'd sold an essay to a slick, I had a book coming out in March.

It was daylight when we landed, daylight and humid. The air wrapped itself around you like the jungle, only here the air was gray and full of dirt. I made my way to a water fountain, found my pack on a revolving carousel, and took the El into the city. I got off at State and Lake and walked up to the Billy Goat Tavern, a journalists' hangout on Michigan. I ordered water and waited for lunch.

The bartender, a fat guy named Nick with a thin mustache and small, narrowly spaced eyes, asked if I was new in town.

"Nope."

"Where you from?"

"Arizona." My parents lived in Arizona.

He said he knew a pretty good barber who could take care of my hair, real cheap. He looked at my gear, dirty and stained from the heat. "You won't get no job," he said, "looking like that."

I said I was almost famous, that I didn't need a job, and asked for another water. From across the room I could hear voices, two men and a woman in tweed talking about Washington and reverse discrimination—city contracts, something about waste removal. Nick leaned over the bar and winked. "Washington," he said, "he's the mayor. And a fine black one at that." He stood back and passed me some peanuts I didn't want. "You like some coffee? More water? You really don't look so good."

"Just the toilet," I said, and he pointed the way.

When I came back I told Nick I knew who Washington was: he was the mayor. What I didn't tell Nick was that the year the people of Chicago elected Washington I almost got married; instead I went to graduate school. Afterwards I was supposed to go to Peru and live in a village—do some fishing, watch the water.

In Chicago the women wore tweed, even in August. I kept

waiting: through the prelunch rush, the lunch rush. I watched men in suits stand up to the bar and drink rum and sodas, martinis, vodka rocks. I tried not to listen and watched the news on an elevated color television; I drank fourteen glasses of water, keeping count with peanuts. At quarter after two she finally showed up and sat at a table with a tall, thin man who might have resembled me had I visited Nick's barber, had I worn a linen suit and said the right things a long time ago.

"Nick," I called. "Send that woman a drink."

"A.T.?" His eyebrows rose, he knuckled his ear.

"Yeah," I said. "The usual."

"Vodka tonic, lemon twist," he said.

"Fine. Send her four. Wait, make it six."

Nick sent her six vodka tonics, each with a lemon twist. She turned, saw me, and brushed the bangs from her eyes: short yellow hair with long bangs, multiple earrings, none of which had a mate. Her friend rose, concern in his eyes mingled with a degree of primal heat which was almost touching, but she put her hand on his, and he sat down.

She came over to the bar where I sat, her walk pleasantly familiar.

"You're a vision of your former self," I said.

"You're a wreck."

"I already told him that," Nick said. "A.T., you don't have to drink all those if you don't want."

"I thought you were in Peru," she said, touching my arm.

I could feel the heat from her fingers. The bar was cold and I was tired. "I never got there," I said. "I went to a fortune-teller day before I left. She told me someday I'd have kids. She said I shouldn't go so I went somewhere else. Now I'm here. Can you put me up?"

She looked over at Nick with his hands spread on the bar, listening.

"Orion," she said, "I'm almost thirty now. I can float you some money, if you want."

I looked at her and said it was nice seeing her again, which was more or less true, but I was angry because I wasn't sure why. I stood and slung the pack over my shoulder, grabbed my gear and a paperback. The weight of the pack made me stagger. I hadn't eaten for three days because nothing stayed in anymore, it just went rushing out like a river, and I could see her eyes—limpid blue, with a new edge of wrinkles running into streams. I could see her eyes darken like a sky with maybe a cloud or two while I wondered why she never saw in me what I wanted to see in her. And then I passed out.

I spent three weeks in a cell in a village north of Matagalpa, twenty-one days. I didn't know it was twenty-one days until Julio fetched me out. He told a Sandanista lieutenant I was a good American and very stupid sometimes, he said he'd take care of me. In the cell I ate dog meat and swallowed rotten water; I picked lice out of my armpits and wished I were in Peru.

"Here," says Julio. "You take my picture. I save you." He is standing four miles inside the Honduras border in front of a burned-out school bus once painted army green: choppers are landing in the distance, slow lumbering bugs with vast metal wings beating the wind, stirring up the dirt and air.

"Put your bandanna on," I say, and he does. He stands in front of me with his M-1 and red mask and looks very proud of something. He is almost eighteen.

Three months later a mortar exploded. It put fragments of a tree inside the back of my head, just above the neck. I woke up alone and lost and took a picture of the field—still smoldering, pits in the black earth turned to mud and shit beneath a yellow-orange haze. There are no corpses, and I remember thinking there should be some.

The church wanted children, lots with big smiles to show at

anti-Contra rallies in the states, where well-intentioned activists would say things like, "In Nicaragua, over half the population is under fifteen." And I found them—there will always be kids who smile, even in Managua—and I told these kids someday they'd be tall like me and run the country if somebody else didn't first. Frankly, I said, it was none of my business. Once I helped three boys fix a tire swing over a stream: the sun is shining through tall green trees with thick leaves and bouncing off the water, and you can see the spray of impact, drops like diamonds scattered in the sun while a boy lands feet first and naked, his hands held high and straight.

While I slept I kept reshooting through all these shadows, one after the other, as if I could only remember each face, each landscape with a lens held up against my eye. But this was nothing new, I always dreamed through the camera. What was new was that I wasn't shooting anything recent, like Nick and his mustache with widespread hands on a fine mahogany bar; like the tall, skinny reporter who might have looked like me if he didn't live in Chicago and cover the Union League; like A.T., blue-eyed and lovely even if now she was almost thirty.

A.T. stood for her name, but I had only known her as Anna; in college she was two years ahead of me and captain of a field hockey team. She didn't become A.T. until she signed on at the *Tribune* and realized her career as a columnist writing on the dilemmas facing single women: Should a woman risk rejection and buy her lover condoms? What type should she buy? What color? She was a writer, she said, and it paid.

As for the guy who looked like me, his name was Harold. I asked him if he was named after his father.

"McClenahan," he said, "are you always such an ass?" He was calling for Anna, for A.T. I'd been here for two days—on the couch, but I didn't tell him that. It wasn't my place.

"I understand there's a lot happening in the Persian Gulf," he said.

I said, "She went out for breakfast. She was hungry."

"Why couldn't you just have lunch?" Harold said, and I hung up. Anna had entered the room and told me to stop running up her phone bill.

I followed her out into a bright room: wood floors, fresh light, a Manet print on the wall, and I drank espresso while she munched on a chocolate croissant. I worked at half a grapefruit and said, "That was Omaha. I've been invited to participate in a big shoot —A Day in the Life of Nebraska."

She kept eating, picking at her croissant as if she was thinking about it. I told her Oak Park suited her fine. "Hemingway lived here," I said. "He wrote for a paper, too. You could be on to something, Anna."

She looked at me, brushed her bangs. "I don't love him, you know. But I want kids now. A lot has changed, Orion. If I don't marry in three years, I'm going to have them myself."

"Yourself?"

"You know what I mean." She arched one of her eyebrows, the way she used to, and asked if I was a father yet. I said I wasn't, but maybe if I was, things would be different.

She shrugged, said, "Maybe. I don't know." She reached over and took what was left of my grapefruit. "You need to gain some weight," she said. "Why'd you come here? Why not home?"

"I like Chicago. I didn't know anyone anywhere else."

She laughed, a little too forcedly, flicked my hand with her wet spoon. "Harold would disapprove," she said, and I wondered just how much Harold could disapprove. I wondered if Harold could in any way be connected with this woman the way I thought I had been.

"Orion," she said, "what are those marks on your neck?"

"What marks?"

"The scars."

"I don't know," I said. "They just showed up one month."

"You don't drink anymore?"

"No."

We went to the Art Institute and sat on some steps looking at Chagall's stained glass mural. Anna said this blue was her favorite, but I already knew that. It was the blue of deep water, old glass, the lambent blue of a dark sky with color. Afterwards we met Harold outside for lunch. I took a picture of Anna and him together underneath a statue of a green lion. "One law for the ox and the lion is oppression," I said.

Harold said, "Cummings?"

"Blake," said Anna.

"Old Peruvian proverb," I said. "If you guys get married, I want to take the pictures. I don't say that to just anyone."

"Who said anything about marriage?" Harold said. He was clearly pleased. I noticed the sleeves of his jacket were a bit short and thought I might buy him some cuff links.

Now we were walking across the street, the traffic busy and fast, and I was thinking about presents when I collided with a bicyclist. A dispatcher in orange and brown. He sent me sprawling into a parked station wagon while Harold and Anna looked on, while the bicyclist himself, a stocky Puerto Rican with a thin beard and probably three kids, picked up his walkie-talkie and told me to get my goddamn ass out of the way.

I hit him, cold-cocked him good. I hit him again, was about to slam his head into the blue sloping curve of a mailbox when Harold grabbed my shoulder. I let go of one, ready to let into another, and saw Anna—eyes wide, insolent—and I knew I wanted to hit her too.

"All he had to do was apologize," I said. "That's all he had to do!"

"He didn't have to do anything!" she screamed. "You ran into him!"

"Jesus Christ," Harold said.

"Jesus Christ died a long fucking time ago." I helped the Puerto

Rican up, said I was sorry, and walked away looking for a post office or bank. Something tall and public.

My parents settled in Sedona, Arizona. Glenn Ford and Henry Fonda filmed a movie there in 1965, *The Rounders,* about old cowboys coping with the new West and an alcoholic horse. As for myself, I grew up fairly well educated and fell in love almost twice. I learned to work with black and white, believing that color stifled the imagination and polluted your vision, the way Henry Fonda and Glenn Ford look green or purple in front of rocks which are supposed to be red—the fine result of iron oxide. That's what makes the cliffs red in Sedona. Iron oxide.

There is this one picture: a girl, almost eight, with missing front teeth, long black hair, a white flower tucked behind her ear; the color of her blouse is the color of her skin, only lighter, and she is puzzled, looking into the camera, a finger raised before her in my direction, only I'm not in the picture. I'm in front of it.

Her mother asks me why I came here; her hair is long and tangled and she is no longer pretty, she may never have been pretty.

"To do some good," I say.

And she says, wiping her hair away from her eyes with the end of a shovel, "I don't think you can do that."

We bury her son after an old priest prays for the corpse; we have to bury it quickly because the sun is hot, Julio has been dead too long. I found him two hundred yards north of the field with no corpses, face down in the Coco, his legs tied to an overhanging branch before someone cut the rope with a machete. You can see the notch in the tree, the rope still wrapped around his legs swimming in the thin muddy water near the bank. There is a rock the size of a bowling ball near his head washed over with blood, and I'm wondering which killed him first, the rock or the river. Now I spend two days looking for a Volkswagen. I drive back and pick up the body, wet and stiff and starting to bloat, covered with flies now like moss on a rock. I take him to his village and give him to his mother, and she says, "I don't think you can do that." She picks splinters out of my head, and I shoot a picture of her daughter, Maria. It's coming out in *Life* next month.

It's all I can remember, these pictures, and the feeling that I shouldn't be where I was. When I left I made my way up the coast, stopping in Acapulco and Manzanillo, Mazatlan only to drink. In Mazatlan I drank myself quiet for a month, avoided the tourists until I was hospitalized and dehydrated. I went to Ensenada where my parents kept a place. There I walked on the beach, whittled sticks with a knife. I read novels and wrote to my mother, said I was fine. My brother had died, I'd missed my father's birthday, and I didn't know where to go.

Harold had called me an ass, and the women in Chicago wore tweed. I spent the day wandering the streets of Chicago wondering what it was I had done in Mexico after leaving Nicaragua. I went to Grant Park, ate part of a soy dog, and photographed two lovers under a tree: behind them stands a man playing an oboe. He has a beard and no shoes, and his hair is as long as mine. The picture is sentimental tripe.

I walked to an El stop and went west to Oak Park. It was late and the train went over its tracks, steady and sure of its pace, taking us through the Projects. During the day they look like fallout shelters no longer useful. The windows are blown out and the bricks which hold them together seem to rot while you watch. Chainlink keeps kids from falling off the sixth or ninth floor, and usually you can see them staring at the train as it goes by, wide-eyed and still very pretty, chocolate and small with tufts of wiry hair.

But now it was dark, and when the train stopped I could see

only myself, my reflection inside this well-lit train and what I was supposed to look like. I watched a short black man enter the car. He wore a long gray coat and no shirt, and his skin was smooth and wet from the heat. I watched him hustle a woman's watch—the shell game:

My name's Stan, and I'm the man;
It ain't no sin if a honky wins,
'Cause I like 'em white and I play all night. . . .

It went on and he was aiming for me now, the watch dangling from his hand. There was another with him, a boy who was supposed to win and prove that I could too. The boy looked like the man, only younger.

The man sat down across from me. I told him I didn't wear a watch.

"That's a fine, fine looking camera."

We played, my camera up against the watch he'd just won and a ten. I picked the right shell, which was really a Dixie cup, and returned the watch to the woman, who put it on her wrist without saying anything. She wore a lime-green scarf which blew in the vent of an air conditioner. The air was hot and the scarf wrapped itself around her throat as if she was a flagpole. "It's okay," I said. "I do this all the time."

Stan was waiting for me, the cups on a box, the box on his knees. "Double or nothing," he said. "Your camera for my forty."

"Let's see your forty," I said.

"Aw, man, my name's Stan! Tell 'em, Boy. Ain't my name Stan? Don't you see me here every night helping folks, helping folks make right and earn some tax-free economies? You ask the boy who I am."

The boy looked up at me and nodded vigorously. "His name Stan," said the boy.

"And I know who—"

"Let's see your forty," I said.

"Now I told you. I told you who I was. I'm Stan, now watch my hand. Watch the cup now. Watch!"

The train stopped, I gave the boy Stan's ten and got off. I could hear the people inside saying something loudly before the doors sealed shut.

The air felt warm and moist. I walked the twenty minutes along sidewalks under tall, swaying oaks. Anna answered the door in her robe and said she was worried. "Where have you been?" she said.

"Where's Harold?"

"We had an argument. You want a drink? Some coffee? I have tea," she said.

She drank a cabernet and fixed me blackberry tea with no caffeine. We sat on her couch and I told her I liked Harold, that he seemed sensible and bright. I don't know if it was true or not, but I wanted to say something. Outside her window we could see a third of the moon and the bloody-gray sky of Chicago at night.

"Why don't you go home?" she said. "It's so pretty there. Your mother called last May and asked if I'd heard from you. She was worried, Orion."

"I spent three weeks in a cell," I said. "It was an open cell, the type with bars made out of wood. Inside were rats, big ones, they'd crawl in at night and chew on your toes if you slept. This lieutenant put me in it, took my papers and told me to have a nice day. He had a mustache and pressed pants. You could see the creases."

She poured more wine and lit a cigarette, passed it to me even though she knew I didn't smoke. I held it between my fingers, and she lit one for herself. "Go on," she said. She wasn't wearing earrings.

"He said he liked me, I looked okay. He brought me a U.S.

Army issue .45 with a live round in the chamber—said this belonged to a Freedom Fighter, that anytime I felt the urge, to go ahead. Go ahead and use it. Sometimes he had the guards give me tequila instead of water."

"But you didn't use it."

"No, I didn't use it. When I got out, he made me take his picture. He saved my camera so I could take his picture. We had a drink in the sun."

She leaned over, set her head in my lap, and I let my fingers run through her bangs. "I think I'm going to move to L.A.," she said, sighing. "I thought you might have changed."

We stayed like this, wandering in the vast space between us, and I wondered if what separated us was what separated everyone; and then she kissed me goodnight and went to bed. I took a shower and looked at a map of Central America. I fell asleep on the couch, the colored ink of another world spread about me like a blanket.

Light wedges through the trees. The lieutenant stands in front of my now-empty cell: he looks very tall and you can see the creases in his khaki slacks. In one hand he holds a riding crop, and in the other, my passport—open so you can see my picture. I don't have a mustache like him, and you can see I look younger than I really am.

"You are too thin for an American," he says.

In the morning, before leaving for her office, Anna fixed coffee and showed me the paper. In the Living section was her weekly column, this one entitled "What Do Old Beaux Do, Anyway?"

I said it looked interesting and went on to the Horoscopes. "Harold's a good guy," I said.

"You keep saying that." She was fixing her tie, thin and red with an oversized shirt she might have picked up at a thrift shop, only I knew she hadn't. I knew that each article she wore now had been carefully selected from a floor at Marshall Field's. She didn't need to buy used clothes anymore, she wrote columns about old lovers and took the train.

She turned and faced me, and I saw that she wore an earring I had given her in college—a small, round pearl. I had asked the salesman if he would sell me only one; he refused, I bought the pair, had my ear pierced and wore the other for two or three months until I lost it. The hole in my ear had long since closed up.

"You should get Harold some cuff links," I said. "They'd go swell with his watch."

"I have to run. If you're going to stay in Chicago, we should find you a place. There's eggs in the fridge," she said. "I'll call for lunch," and she shut the door.

She returned a few moments later, went to the coffee table and picked up her keys: she is leaning over it, her bangs hanging low at the same degree as her red tie which grazes the fine wood of the table, the yellow hair sweeping the blue of her eyes which you can't quite see, and she is saying, to me, to some man out of her past who she just doesn't know anymore, "I forgot these."

Now she blows a kiss to her sun room where I sit drinking her coffee and watching, and she leaves.

————————

I had a series coming out in less than a month, I had a book due in March. My father had another ten years or so left. Things, I thought, will always get worse.

I picked up the phone and called Sedona collect. I told my father happy birthday, that I was sorry for waking him. He said, "No problem, Cass," and I asked him to put Mom on.

"Mom," I said, "I'm fine. I'm in Chicago, on my way to Omaha." I told her I'd been in Dublin, on a walking tour, that I went only where it was safe. I told her I was going to take pictures of Nebraska. She said she was glad to hear it and started to cry.

"Mom," I said, "don't do that. Everything's smooth. Smooth as ice." My brother Cass used to say this often, and she began to cry more.

After a while I said I could stand some money, two or three grand if it was handy. This cheered her up, she said she'd wire five. "The view here is lovely," she said. "Send us some pictures."

My family is Irish, steeped in its history and vice; we drink too much, we fight too much. While I cleaned Anna's kitchen, I ate an apple with two slices of Muenster cheese. I listened to Vivaldi and tried not to think about my family. My father, I knew, would be at Boynton Canyon later in the day, riding his horse, Cleo. My mother might walk the dog, an arthritic setter, down to the creek where she'd let him splash in the water. Maybe my parents would go out to dinner to talk about me.

When the dishes were dry, I packed up and walked to the train. The ride into the city was crowded and full of people who owned more things than I wanted to carry. After I picked up my money, I went to a camera shop and bought twenty rolls, just in case. I left the store and walked on up to the Billy Goat.

Anna was waiting for me at the bar, and Nick wore the same mustache and shirt. He pretended not to recognize me.

Anna looked at my gear. "What's this?" she said.

"I decided to get an early start."

"On what?"

"If I knew that, I would have started earlier."

Nick slid me a glass of water, passed me the peanuts. I drank half the water down and pushed the peanuts aside.

"What do you do," I whispered, "when it all goes away?"

She looked across the room, sipped at her drink.

"What do you do when you don't know what you want to do anymore?"

"I don't know," she said. "Join a health club?"

I finished my water, and she reached for me. "I don't know, Orion. I really don't know."

"Well I do. I know what you do. You go south, Anna. You get yourself on a plane and you go to Peru."

"Peru?"

"Peru," I said. "Be sure to write."

———————

Michigan Avenue: I know the street, I knew the town. My mother had raised me and my brother in a Chicago suburb while my father worked in the city like everyone else. On St. Patrick's Day, before he got really drunk, he'd take us into Chicago and show us the river. "Look," he'd say, "that's the river. That's the Chicago River, Boys. See how it's green? It's green because Mayor Daley is Irish, because every St. Patrick's Day he turns it green. In honor of him, St. Pat." Eventually, my father and mother settled in Sedona, and once, in Berkeley, I went to a palm reader with a girl I didn't know very well. I don't know what happened to her, either.

I crossed the river over the Michigan bridge where the water is green and thick and three hundred feet below me. I can smell the water and feel the traffic make the bridge sway, feel the cement and steel flex with each passing axle under my toes. The water is straight down and steep, and I think about letting go: setting the camera free and watching it and the red strap sail down through the air, slowly, greeting the water with hardly a splash. The slightest of ripples.

I hold the camera out front, arms straight over the water with a wide-angle facing me. My hair is long and muddy-black, my glasses small round circles because for this shot I don't have to take them off. My skin is smooth and my cheeks are neither full nor empty. I look sure of something, a little like my brother, and know the light is right: *hold, still,* a passing breath before you squeeze and feel the shutter click. There is a long silver bus, passing behind me, all a blur.

JET STREAM

Betsy, 1980

I don't like to clean the pool, but that's what I'm doing. Norm says people like to swim in clean water; you can tell it's clean, he says, when it's blue. I push the broom along the floor of the pool and watch the dirt stir and whirl like dust devils. Norm is my stepdad.

He's out here on the lawn reading *Time*, backwards, saving the important stuff for last. He looks fat out here: his paunch is really big like he's pregnant, but it's just full of beer and some of Mom's old cooking. I cook for him now, Swansons and Stouffers.

I go over to the engines and set the pool on Backwash, when Norm starts to laugh. The magazine rattles and the chair wobbles; he's really laughing hard. To clean the filter, you have to run the water through backwards, so I turn the handle, flip the switch and listen to the filter whine like the jumbo jets at the airport. The water goes *swoosh* and starts to flood the river-rock behind the putting green. The putting green has nine holes and little red flags.

"What's so funny?" I say, because Norm is still laughing.

"Carter," Norm says. "He's not going to let us go to the Olympics if Russia keeps screwing around in Afghanistan. Now that's what I call effective foreign policy." He says *effective* like he's from a farm, but he's not. "What the hell have you got on?" he says.

He means my shorts: they're really Ruth's and have orange and blue polka dots, and I'm wearing my big white tank top—the one Mom wouldn't let me wear because you can see everything through the armholes. Sometimes I catch Norm taking looks, but this is still my favorite shirt. I like the way it fits so loose. Eric says it's his favorite, but he only wants me to wear it around him. When I graduate, Eric wants to go to New York or Los Angeles with me and become a studio musician.

"Miss Crocker," says Norm, "would you be so kind as to bring me a beer?" He calls me Crocker after the company, Betsy Crocker, but the real name's Betty. My name is Betsy.

"How come the water looks so green?" I say.

"Too many chemicals, that's all. There's some in the vegetable bin."

I leave the water running over the river-rock and go in to get Norm a beer, and he yells, "I hope someone gave you those!"—referring to the shorts. Clyde, my Irish wolfhound, is lying on the floor underneath the kitchen table; his tail sways back and forth to keep him cool. Norm won't run the air-conditioning anymore except at night to sleep. The house is too big, he says, and we don't use enough of it anyway. I go to the garage where he keeps the beer because I know there's only one in the vegetable bin. I open a case and take out eight or nine, the cans on top my arms like sticks. I bring them inside and put them in the freezer so they'll get cold quick. I give Clyde an oatmeal cookie, but he's not hungry. It just sits by his nose while he thinks.

Last night when Eric came over he was still in his ARCO shirt with *Harry* ironed over the pocket. The pockets are always streaked with ink from his pens going in and out, and he smelled like mechanic's soap and sweat. The soap smells like plastic and makes his hands dry. Norm called him Harry, trying to be funny, and he asked how much for a tune-up.

"I don't know, Norm."

Eric's been working on the corner of Twenty-fourth and Camelback for a year waiting for me to finish school. I put the beers from the vegetable bin in my knapsack and we left. I kept one out, held it between my legs while I hung on to Eric, while we cruised on his Kawasaki looking for something. At stoplights I'd hold the beer up for him and pour. The night was hot and dry, but you don't notice the heat if you're moving, with the wind whipping your hair and the steady rumbling of the motorcycle going beneath you making your legs sweat against the seat.

We went down Central but saw no one we knew: just the regulars with their hopped-up cars, sometimes their parents' cars. We drove all the way to South Mountain. From on top of South Mountain you can see all of Phoenix. The lights spread out into stars and never stop. You can see them forever up there. We drank the warm beers and sat on a big rock. There were cars next to us, some girl was yelling at her boyfriend. The other cars were silent except for one that was running so its air-conditioning could stay on. We sat outside and Eric looked at the stars while I looked at his hands, at the black grease under his fingernails and his leather knuckles. Inside, the palms are rough and full of calluses. He says the only way to get them really clean is to use a toothbrush, and I held his hands with mine and thought about the way they felt so that later I'd remember it—the feeling with the air and the lights and the heat, the sound of the car running to keep cool.

When we got home Norm was asleep on the couch, the house felt cold. Cal Worthington was selling cars with his dog, Spot, and a beer had spilled from Norm's lap and soaked the carpet. I threw the can away. I took off his shoes and covered him with the sheet he keeps at the end of the couch. I turned the volume down, but left the TV on just in case.

Clyde was waiting for us on my bed, and Eric threw him off.

"Eric," I said, "if you're not nice to Clyde, he won't be nice to you."

And he said, "For Christ's sake, Betsy. It's just a dog."

I put Clyde outside and brushed my teeth while Eric thought about things. Sometimes Eric gets mean when he drinks and wants to fight, but not now. Now he was thinking. He thinks a lot, just lies and stares at the ceiling and thinks. He says thinking is good for musicians, that I should think more. But I don't like to think, I just like to know how things feel.

And then we started doing it, like we usually do, on the big bed Mom gave me when I turned fifteen before I knew Eric. We were going along pretty nice for a while, but then he stopped right in the middle and picked me up so I'd be on top. He didn't even say anything. He just stopped and did that.

I'm at the piano working my way through the second movement of the *Appassionata* when Ruth comes over. I forgot about Norm's beer, but when he came in he said it sounded good. Sometimes he's nice to me to make himself feel better.

"It's in the freezer," I said, "getting cold."

"I'm going to take a shower. Cool off."

Norm showers a lot lately. He doesn't like swimming. The week after the insurance was due, his music store burned down. He said he was busy with other things and forgot. When my brother Kevin got married in Dallas, Mom said that was it. "I've had it," she said. Mom was my teacher, the *Appassionata* my last assignment. She said I wasn't ready for the *Waldstein*, but Norm says I can do whatever I want. "You know what you want to do," he says, "and you do it."

"Just like that?"

And he says, "Yes."

Once he told me he wished I really was his daughter, and he started crying. My real father lives in California. I told Norm it was okay, and let him hold me while he cried and got my hair wet. This was after Mom had sent a postcard from New Orleans where she said it was humid. Later the Arizona Bank sent a letter to Norm—a notice of foreclosure—and Norm wadded it up into a ball. He threw it across the putting green for Clyde to fetch, and Clyde brought it back. Norm kept throwing and Clyde kept fetching until the wind picked it up and carried the wadded ball into the pool with Clyde's slobber skimming all around. Clyde stood on the deck waiting for it to float in reach.

I hear him barking at Ruth's moped, that's how I know it's her. Today she's wearing white cotton shorts with big pockets and my red No Nukes T-shirt. Her hair is jet black and she has these big almond eyes and a wide mouth. Her skin is perfect and tan, we lie out by the pool a lot with our shirts off. Neither of us shaves because that's not what they do in Europe. Ruth is really beautiful.

"You weren't at school," she says.

"Overslept."

We go into the kitchen for iced tea and look out the window into the yard. The pool is half-empty, the putting green floats under three or four inches of water: ankle-deep. Norm's lawn chair lies on its side, the magazine is soaked, the little red flags with numbers look like they've sunk. Clyde is out there jumping and splashing in the water looking for fish.

Ruth and I, we just stand and watch. Finally she touches my hand: tears are leaking out of her almond-shaped eyes filled with what's inside her—we're never sure what, exactly, but we know it's in there and important like the way things happen in a dream.

"My grandmother wants me to come to L.A.," she says.

And I think this is something I already know how to do, something I'm already getting pretty good at.

Ruth used to sleep with Mr. Fennerstrom, our history teacher. He was still pretty young and wore a beard, and he'd talk to our class as if we really mattered. He told us why Jerry Garcia was important and why John Travolta wasn't. He told us stories about when he was in Ohio protesting the Vietnam war. He told us the Palo Verde nuclear plant would destroy the desert and all of us around it, and he had us write letters to the *Gazette* and the *Republic* instead of reports. They never printed any, but Mr. Fennerstrom said they wouldn't, and he said if people stopped driving there wouldn't be a gas shortage.

Once he took me and Ruth to a Jackson Brown concert at Arcosanti in Cordes Junction. The people had parked their cars in grass and someone's muffler caught it on fire. Cars started blowing up and the concert had to stop. On the way home, we stopped at Ferrells for ice cream. It was a lady's birthday and the hostess banged a drum while a boy with acne and a black garter around his arm honked a brass horn. We all sang happy birthday to the lady, laughing and making shapes with our ice cream, our spoons like big safe chisels. We had a huge mound of Pistachio and Almond Cream in one bowl between us, and this was how we ate it. After Mr. Fennerstrom dropped me off at my house, he drove Ruth to the school parking lot where she left her moped. Ruth says that's when they kissed, in the parking lot outside like he was just another football player or wrestler, though we never go out with jocks. At first it made me jealous.

On one hand he had only three fingers, and he would keep

them curled like a loose fist so you wouldn't notice. Once, when he was talking about nuclear energy, he explained what could happen. "It only takes one mistake," he was saying. "One little mistake, one little slip and oops—she'll blow like a whale."

I was thinking about the last movement of the *Appassionata*, how if you slipped up the first arpeggios the whole piece would tumble down inside your head and you'd never find your way out.

"One mistake," he said. "How many of you have ever made a mistake? Just one little mistake?" He stopped pacing and pulled on his beard, looking thoughtful while we all sat and wondered what mistake of ours was the worst, or which one everyone knew the most about. After he and Ruth started it all, he wouldn't look at me in class; he'd get nervous sometimes when I asked questions. But today he looked up, stopped tugging on his beard, with his good hand, and turned right to me. He shrugged his shoulders and said as if he were sad, "I rest my case."

It was strange knowing Mr. Fennerstrom like that: I knew all about him through Ruth, and I know he knew all about me, but it was as if we knew all these things, these secrets, without ever knowing them. They were just there, like air or the mail at your front door each morning waiting to be gone through.

Last December before he killed himself, Mr. Fennerstrom wrote Ruth a letter explaining it wasn't her fault, that it was his own fault and he alone was responsible for him just like Ruth was for her. He said the whole thing had nothing to do with her, but he forgot to mail the letter, or maybe he decided not to mail it and forgot to throw it out. His landlord found the letter in a drawer and gave it to the police, who gave it to the papers. The papers printed it, everything, the stuff about how he thought about her in class, the Jackson Brown concert and me, *the pianist with promise*—even the way he signed it at the end: *Love, Fenny*. Mr. Buckner said he was going to throw Ruth out of school. "For her own sake," Ruth said. But he never did. Miss Williams and some others said she was a strong girl and seemed to be handling the situation okay. Ruth told me Mr. Fenner-strom was wrong, though, that it was everyone's fault—hers, Mr. Buckner's, Miss Williams'. Even mine.

None of the girls at school talk to Ruth anymore because everyone loved Mr. Fennerstrom. The guys all think she's a slut; even Eric tried to hit on her, but he thinks I don't know. The guys at school all know she knows more than any of them, they won't talk to her in front of any of the girls, and now she tells me her grandmother wants her to come live in L.A. Her foster parents think it's a good idea.

"It *was* their idea," she says.

We're outside now, I've shut off the pump. We walk through the water over the prickly grass. Clyde barks and he wants to play. I uncoil the hose, put it in the half-empty pool to fill it up. The metal end scrapes on the sides, and Ruth turns the water on.

"Do you think Norm will be mad?" she says.

The way Mr. Fennerstrom killed himself was: he drove off a cliff north of Phoenix near Camp Verde on Christmas Eve. "So everyone would think it was an accident," Ruth said. "He talked about it once. He didn't want to hurt anybody's feelings."

"Ruth," I say, "let's go somewhere."

She looks at me the way she does sometimes, and I say, "It doesn't matter. I just feel like going."

When you ride with Eric, you feel the bones and muscles inside his back, the long *V* leading up to his shoulders. Everything feels tight and in place like where it should. But it's different with Ruth, she doesn't feel the same. Her skin feels soft even through my No Nukes T-shirt and I can smell her soap, Dove. Her moped goes slow and putters loud when she tries to go fast. Together we weight too much for it, but this is the way we go.

The Burger King is first. We drink Tab and look out the window, and you can see our reflection.

"The airport," Ruth says.

She means Sky Harbor where they're building a new terminal. Sometimes we hang out at the airport. We watch people come and go, wave, say hello or hug and cry. In Phoenix all the cowboys except for Norm go to the airport. You never see them on the streets, only in the terminals with new hats and boots with reptile skin. They're always going home, too. To Minnesota or Milwaukee. At night sometimes we go out on the runway and feel the jets land.

"This was my year for Beethoven," I say. "Mom said she'd finish me off with Liszt, the *Mephisto Waltz*. She said then I'd be ready for anything."

"Who's Liszt?"

"Nineteenth century. When Liszt was little, Beethoven heard him play. After, Beethoven went and picked him up and told him someday he'd be famous."

Mom used to tell me these stories. Mom used to be famous, before she married my dad, when she played everywhere. My dad makes movies and says I don't have to worry about college, that it's all taken care of, even though I haven't seen him since I was six. Ruth doesn't know any of the names but she says she likes to hear me play. She likes Chopin and Brahms. She likes it when I play "Rootbeer Rag" by Billy Joel. Mom said my hands are too small for me to be great. She said it's all in the hands and some people's are smaller than other's. My fingers are too short, but Mom says I use them right. "You know where to put them," she says. "You have your father's hands."

"I hate her," I say, sounding it out.

"Let's go to the airport."

We don't want another Tab, but I still have to fix dinner. I walk over to a pay phone and call Angeleno's. I order Norm a big one with extra cheese, with pepperoni and mushrooms.

Laconic—it's a word Mr. Fennerstrom made me look up. It means quiet and sometimes rude because you don't talk much; it means *terse*. I had to look *terse* up to find out exactly what *laconic* means, and that's what Eric is. He doesn't talk much, he sits and thinks. He broods. Ruth doesn't talk much either, but she's not *laconic*. With Ruth I always know what she's thinking. It doesn't matter if she doesn't talk. Sometimes we both don't talk, we just know and listen to each other. Ruth is more like *pithy*, which sounds worse than it is.

We ride out to the airport, down Twenty-fourth past the ARCO station. Eric's standing outside leaning on one of the pumps with a sign that says *No Unleaded*. He's thinking about something and doesn't see us, and there's a lot of traffic so we don't have to worry about going slow, or not going fast enough. The sun is setting, turning the sky all sorts of colors: purple and green and orange, a little red before it smears into soft thick clouds. In Phoenix you feel like you need an ocean when you watch the sunset. The sky is pretty and it's hot and long green palm trees are everywhere, but there's still no ocean.

A car full of Mexicans speeds up and then slows beside us. They yell something in Spanish and their voices go really high, and Ruth tells them to *fuck off!* This makes them yell more and we're coming up to a light—yellow. The Mexicans stop and we go on through. A truck carrying dirt with a tractor hooked up behind honks, but you can tell by the look on the guy's face he's not really mad.

———

It's dark now, the colors in the sky are gone and you can't see any stars. The smog is bad. We climb over a tall chainlink fence with no barbwire, but Ruth hooks the pocket of her shorts at the top. This scares her, and she starts to scramble and shake like she's getting tired of holding herself up there.

"Wait," I say, climbing higher. I reach my hand up to help, but

I can't unhook the cloth.

"Rip it," she says, shaking.

That's what I do—I rip it and cut three inches of the pocket. Ruth swings over and climbs down, and I follow. When we're on the ground we both lean against the fence, breathing. My heart is going fast, and Ruth looks at the tear in her shorts. Her legs are tan and make the shorts look white even in the dark.

In front of us is the runway with big arrows and lines painted on in between all the low blue lights. The lights are neon-blue and close to the ground. We walk a while and stop before we get too far. We wait, our arms stretched out with our hands holding onto the warm blue lights. The lights are glowing and color our arms. Between Ruth and me is a light, our fingers overlap while we tense our arms, waiting.

We hear the jet, see the large wings like shadows pulling it down as if gravity really does work, gliding in slow and easy as a goose on water. We feel the pull and heat and feel our legs rise, straight out behind us, hovering like the plane while our bodies get swept up in the afterwash. We're levitating, our fingers touching, with the roar of gas and wind and air blowing through our ears and sucking at us, pulling and making us want to stop because our arms keep shaking. Our legs rise and we float with our eyes closed tight, feeling the jet and the wings, the air making so much noise it almost hurts.

Our ears ring in the silence. We're waiting for another. It's strange the way everything seems so quiet when everything feels so loud.

"This will make you deaf," Ruth says.

"Like Beethoven," I say.

"How'd he do that, anyway?"

It's not really a question, but it was all in his hands. "The Ninth came from his fingertips," I say.

"It'll still make you deaf," Ruth says, but I can't really hear because another plane is coming in from somewhere and we're being sucked up into its space the way it's being sucked into ours. I'm wondering what I'm going to do when Ruth's gone, and she's wondering the same. But we aren't talking about that because we're in a vacuum. We're holding onto blue lights in the dark. We're in the jet stream.

When you fly into Phoenix at night, the first things you watch are the same lights you see from on top of South Mountain. I've never flown in at night, but Ruth has, and she says the view is the same.

Eric's motorcycle is parked in the driveway and we hear Fleetwood Mac playing. Ruth parks the moped by the gate leading to the backyard where Norm and Eric sit in lawn chairs in the water on the putting green drinking beer. The pool is flooded, filled to the top and running into the water on the grass, and Clyde is lying on top of the diving board where it's dry even though he's all wet. Norm's wearing the Bermudas I gave him last Christmas, Eric's in his jeans, and you can tell they're both pretty drunk and have been swimming or trying to play golf.

"They took the car," Norm says.

"Who?"

"The repossession men, that's who. Didn't even bother to ask for the keys. I would have given them the keys if they asked. But they didn't even ask. They just came and took the car."

"You said that," Eric says. And then, looking at me, "Where have you been?" He looks mean, the way he does when he's worked too long at the station and it's hot, the way he does when other guys look at me.

"Nowhere," I say.

"Goddamnit—"

"Hey," says Norm. "Hey. Just hey—"

"Where the hell have you been?"

Norm stands up and tips over the lawn chair. His shorts are wet and glow under the porch lights. "Eric," he says, "you may very well—" He stops, looks at me. "You may—" Now he's look-ing for a cigarette. "But I'll not abide your talking to my Betsy that way." He looks serious, even if he is wobbling and digging through his wet pockets.

"Is there any pizza left?" I ask, watching Ruth shut off the hose. I see her go inside before I can tell her not to.

"He gave it to the dog," Eric says.

"Did no such thing."

Eric stands, turns so that he's facing me. "I won't ask you again," he says.

"Does it matter? What does it matter?"

"It matters 'cause I want to know!"

He's not looking at me, he's looking at my shirt. He's looking at me the way he did last night after he threw Clyde off the bed and got tired of thinking.

"Why don't you just leave? Would you please just leave!"

I'm crying and Norm looks at me, then Eric. Then me. He starts to clap, his hands echoing in the dark with the music playing.

"Wish I'd said the same thing," he says.

Now Eric looks confused, like Clyde when you pretend to throw the ball but don't. Clyde's on the diving board, his tail thumping. Above us is the moon, bright as a floodlight, and I'm still crying, wishing Norm had said the same thing. To Mom so she'd know how we really feel.

———————

Mom used to say if you tried to think too much about it, you'd never stretch and everything would come out the way it was on paper and not the way it was in you. Ruth and I sit on the kitchen floor eating Nachos and drinking warm beer from the garage. Norm has thrown the table into the swimming pool; he's thrown in the chairs and microwave.

He started first by ripping off the speakers from the wall outside and throwing them in the water, one at a time. Fleetwood Mac went from stereo to mono to nothing. Now you hear Norm's panting, sometimes Clyde's bark.

Norm walks by with the television. It's heavy and his face is red, and he says, "You girls gonna help or not?"

I look at Ruth, who can't help laughing. "Sure," I say.

The piano is next. Norm opens up the sliding glass doors and we three get behind to push. The brass wheels stick in the carpet, and Ruth kicks the piano bench over, spilling the music inside. There are some old letters and Christmas cards, a picture of Mom. Norm takes the picture of Mom and sticks it under his arm while we all push.

Outside we have to lift it over the curb of the pool deck, but once over we're ready to go. The piano is a Baldwin baby grand, but out here by the pool under the porch lights and moon it looks like any other baby grand.

We push on *Three!* and the narrow tail falls first. We push again and watch it go. It almost floats before sinking to the bottom with its lid just above the swelling water. Clyde jumps on top and looks over the edge like it's a pier, and Norm throws in the picture of Mom.

Now we do the couch and all the paperbacks from all the bookshelves. I get the weed eater and Ruth takes the vacuum cleaner. We do the lawn furniture and the toilet seat and all the soap and shampoo in the second bathroom. We do the two easy chairs Mom picked out and a lamp.

"Too bad Eric's not—" and Norm stops, remembering why Eric's not here.

"Hey," says Ruth, "it's looking pretty full."

"Wait," says Norm. "I'll get the camera!"

Ruth and I and Clyde sit in front on the piano with our feet wet. Norm is setting the flash and timer, adjusting the tripod and focus. "Okay," he says, and comes running around. He stands on the piano behind us and almost falls in. We smile and Norm says, "Be sure to wave, Girls."

We wave, Norm takes the camera off the tripod. "What the hell," he says, and throws the tripod in on top of the couch. He looks it over a while, taking it in. Finally, he fakes a yawn and says, "Think I'm gonna hit the hay."

On his way to the bedroom we see Norm stop in the kitchen and take three beers. Clyde follows, goes into the house; he pauses to shake off the water in his fur. He's going to go to my room and leap on top the brass bed Mom bought me and wait. Norm will have to sleep in his bed tonight because the couch is already in the pool. Next week Ruth will be sleeping in a guest room at her grandmother's house and the bank will have taken ours away. But right now we're sitting cross-legged on the water in a pool full of stuff.

It's really late, after three. We drink more beer and sit on the piano. We smoke and throw the butts in the pool. We keep the beer from getting hot by holding it in the water, though the water's not cold. Sometimes we flick a splash away and listen to the noise.

"Do you miss him?" I ask.

Ruth thinks for a second and sips her beer. "No," she says. "After a while he was just like everyone else. I was just like everyone else, only younger."

Eric tried to hit on Ruth at a party. He wasn't even drunk, and he told her he wanted to know what she'd be like. Ruth said he wanted to compare. Ruth said he was like everyone after Mr. Fennerstrom, even like her uncle, the one in California. She told Eric she wouldn't tell but she did. We tell each other everything except for the times when we don't have to. For instance, I know why she doesn't want to go back to California.

"You know you're depressed," I say, "when you think you aren't but should be."

"Huh?"

"You know, when you think about it too much."

"I'm not going to go," she says. "I'll run away first."

Overhead the stars are brighter than the lights of Phoenix, but you still can't see them. We used to go swimming a lot: during the day when Norm wasn't around, or sometimes late at night. It was always best at night with a bright moon like now. The water felt more cool and clean and made your hair feel heavier than it really was. You could feel the sky and if you turned the light on it lit up the pool from below and you could see your shadow swimming along beneath. If you dove down and swam near the light, you could feel the heat from the bulb in the cool water. I remember once, before Mr. Fennerstrom and everything—I remember us in the pool. Ruth was glowing in the light under the water because we still weren't that tan. We didn't even have any lines, and her skin was white and perfect and she said I looked *luminous*, like it was me who was making the light. Ruth, she says she's not going to go, but I already know this. I know this the way I know it wasn't me making the light. The way I know no one feels like we feel when the wind is really blowing hard.

BALLISTICS

Michael, 1981

Picture this guy in long Hawaiian shorts, white high-tops and no shirt in the heat of New England summer: flying red hair, red as tomatoes on a vine, long and curly on his head, flying with his body going up and down, side to side. He's in the middle of this wide green lawn, dancing. I don't know what he's dancing to, he wears a personal stereo unit probably made in Taiwan. The music looks loud with two tiny black dots in his head funneling the noise through his head while this guy dances in the middle of a wide lawn. He doesn't dance very well, and he looks as if he might be wishing for rain—the way he moves like Indians on TV, in a circle, spinning around and around up and down with his hair and knees flying out like that. If you look too long, you might get dizzy.

I'm waiting for my friend Don and watching this kid dance. Don called up this morning, said if I had nothing better to do he'd like to go shooting. Don carries some nice guns.

I really can't believe the way this guy keeps hopping around. You'd think he'd get hot and want a Coke. You'd think the music would stop and he'd look around and feel stupid.

Don shows up in his '71 Chevelle; I can tell it's him by the way it sounds. He calls this a man's car. "Get into a man's car," he'll say. He's wearing a camouflage cap he picked up in Hartford, no shirt, and his hunting vest. He's originally from Augusta. He runs a bar on weekends and complains because it's so quaint. Me, I keep the greens for a prep school; I cut grass, I keep the edges sharp. It's what I always say.

"What's that fool doing?" Don says.

"Exercise," I say. "He's doing exercise."

"Looks to me like he's dancing," Don says, getting out of the car. He's wearing khaki slacks and red sneakers. His eyes are shot and the cap on his head leans crooked, to the side like it's on purpose.

"Hey, hey you there! Come here, Boy!"

The kid keeps dancing.

"He can't hear you, Don. Guys with red hair hear bad. Everyone knows that."

But Don's already moving, heading straight for the kid. His walk is heavy and slow, like he's on wet sand and not the smooth grass I cut yesterday morning. He stops short about five feet from the kid, pulls a flask from his hip, sucks on the end and wipes his mouth.

He's too far away for me to hear what he says, but I figure he says something. The kid keeps dancing and Don reaches inside his vest. I see the ten-and-half-inch barrel first—a .45 Magnum, single action and chrome, filled with bullets Don makes in the basement of the house he and his wife rent. He keeps the first chamber empty; for safety, he says. The chrome glimmers and shines. I see the smoke before I hear its shot, up into the sky through a fat white cloud. A gun like that can make the sky rain hard.

The kid isn't dancing anymore. I'm leaning on the hood of Don's car feeling the heat and watching them both. The kid has this weird look on his face, and Don is smiling. Between them both is the chrome barrel of a gun which might as well be stuck with the hot end in the kid's throat.

He never went to Nam. It's not like this is television and he has an excuse to go around threatening people with guns. He flunked out of a university in Georgia and got married. His wife, Janet, was friends with mine before she moved out West. To California, I think.

My wife left the night before Christmas Eve. She'd spent the day baking cookies and spraying the tops with pink and green frosting. We were out of red. Outside was snow and I came in with snow all over my dungarees and she watched me wipe my feet like she always did—for winter, I take care of the hockey rinks, smooth the ice—but she didn't say anything. She just stood there with her arms in the sink, yellow gloves up to her elbows, scrubbing dishes. Her hair hung over her eyes and I couldn't see what she was thinking, and I got this little rumble—just a little one, a hint of weather, but that's all. I thought, Now why doesn't she say something?

Then she did. She asked in this real soft pretty voice of hers how the roads were. I said they weren't too bad, and she said we'd have a nice white Christmas.

"We sure will," I said. I went over to the easy chair, sat back and lit a smoke while she washed dishes. When I woke, the cigarette had burnt itself out, still in my hand; the dishes were in the sink and she was gone.

Janet said it was too bad and asked me over for New Year's. Don and I drank Scotch and watched one of his kids play with a train set he bought secondhand from one of the White Hart regulars. The train made smoke that was supposed to look like steam and the whistle wouldn't work. It went around the Christmas tree in circles, one at a time.

Later Don took me to the basement where he kept his things. On the wall near a red oil furnace hung his guns—no locks, just guns: Smith and Wessons, Colts, two Brownings and a Luger from a dead German his father found in Normandy. He took down a Ruger .357 Magnum, checked the cylinder even though he knew it was clean, and handed it to me.

"You're going to want this," he said.

I looked at him and wondered what he meant.

"In case she ever comes back."

But she never did come back, and the heat from the gun made my hand feel warm.

It's bright and hot. Don's guiding this kid to the car, prodding him this way and that, trying to be friendly. The kid has his hands in the air, but he doesn't look worried. In fact, he's smiling, and saying things like, "Hey, Dude, don't shoot." He says, "It's cool, I'm cool. Sure is a nice cool day."

I've seen the kid but he doesn't know me. His name is Cass. Cass McClenahan. His tuition costs about three thousand more than my salary.

Don puts the gun in his vest and says, "It sure is."

I light a cigarette and watch the kid: he's older than I thought, old enough to drive, and he has bright green eyes. Don pulls out his flask and passes it around. The kid waves it by and asks what time it is.

"Time for a shoot," says Don. "What d'ya say, Red. Up to shooting some?"

The kid digs in his pocket and takes out a mechanical pencil filled with stuff that looks like flour; he digs again and pulls out a little spoon the same color as Don's single action: shiny. He snorts, wipes his nose and says, "What time is it?"

I look up at the sky and measure the sun, but I can't be precise.

_____

The kid wears purple shoelaces and sits in the back with Don's guns, rocking and swaying, the earphones on his head again. You can hear some of the music leak out around the Styrofoam pads, and it sounds thin and hollow, like a radio in a beer can might. When the kid sings along, he sounds as if he's somewhere else. We drive to Millerton for sandwiches, stop first at a Cumby Farms to get some beer. The way I see it, we need to slow the drunk, keep it steady.

There's a big hole in Don's dash where his stereo used to be. If his stereo were here, the kid wouldn't have to listen to his earphones. But the stereo is gone. "Thieves in Maryland," Don said. On his window is a sticker that reads _Jensen_. I told Don if he didn't have that sticker on his window, the thieves in Maryland would have never known he had a stereo.

"Naw," he said. "I put that up after they took it."

_____

We're parked at a drive-through. Don's sucking away on his flask, ordering in between thoughts cheeseburgers and fries; he talks to the machine and lets it take our order. At the window, a girl hands him a sack and says something.

"What?"

"Eight-fifty, please."

She turns away to help someone else—to go to the restroom, mop the dining area. We wait while Don holds his eight-fifty in his hand looking at it. Seventeen years later, we hear someone inside yell, "What's he waiting for?"

And Don says, "Excuse me?"

Another girl with stringy hair comes over. Her smock is dirty and she's leaning on the metal ledge. "Your car's too loud," she says.

"What?"

"What do you want!"

And Don says, looking at the money, "Nothing." He pulls the car into gear, we lurch off, Don saying, "Good Goll A'mighty," and me laughing. Don doesn't curse, and the kid doesn't know he's eating for free; I figure later it wouldn't matter much to him anyway. I gave the kid a cheeseburger with a leaking tomato, and after a while we could hear him chewing as we drove into the woods looking for a place.

"Nothing," I said after a while, which made Don and me laugh all over again.

———————

I don't know why my wife left. But she was a pretty girl with nice smooth legs and none of the veins showing yet. She was a little younger than me; we got married because I made her pregnant, but it was never born. Her skin was always kind of pale like the redheaded kid in back. Sarah, she used to say people with fair skin burn easy, with this voice she said she got from her mother, and I really can't figure out why she went to California. In California people grow their hair long and eat raw fish, they go to San Francisco. I don't even know anyone in California. I don't even know if she went there.

"If I were her," I say, "I would have gone to New Hampshire."

"Where her folks live," Don says.

"Yeah, her mom."

Don pulls into a dirt road, trees tall on the sides, and drives for a while. "Maybe she did," he says.

"She would have told Janet."

He stops the car and swings out. In front of us is a fence of logs to stop cars and a large empty field with short, stubby grass. The grass is yellow because there hasn't been much rain and it's not watered regularly. Here and there are tree stumps from the '50s. Before the trees were cut down, there wasn't any grass.

The kid gets out and helps carry things, the cooler and guns, the ammunition, the lawn chairs, a transistor radio. The kid's finished his cheeseburger and looks as if he's slowing down. I ask him if he wants a beer or something, but he says no.

"She never even finished the dishes," I say, setting up my chair, remembering. "Left nine weeks of laundry piled in the hamper."

"And she forgot to feed the dog."

The dog ran away because I wouldn't feed it anymore. It was her dog, and I don't know where it went, either.

If you take two beefeater tomatoes, set them up, and if you shoot a .22 at one, the bullet will go right on through. It'll pierce the tomato and leave a small clean hole the size of the kid's pencil. But if you take a .45 automatic, and if you hit it, you'll blast that other tomato to pulp—blow it all over everywhere and plant its seeds. First, you've got to know how to aim.

"Do you know how to shoot?" Don asks.

"Sure," says the kid. "My old man drove a tank."

He's helping Don spread a tarp to catch empty rounds: it's six feet square and orange, and sometimes makes a canopy in Don's backyard where he and Janet and the kids and me will sit under it drinking lemonade or beer. Normally I sit with them a lot.

"You've got to let Sarah go," Janet said once. The kids had gone to bed, and we were watching the sky. Sometimes you can see satellites.

"Why?" I said. "Why?"

"Don, honey, you tell him."

But Don just sat there on his lawn chair underneath the orange tarp. I lit a smoke and thought about things.

"You know," Don said, after a while, "I think if it rained, we'd all still get good and wet."

That night I went home thinking about rain. When it rains, the grass is too wet to cut, and I usually paint walls inside the school; sometimes I move dormitory furniture around the campus in a truck. When it rains, the White Hart gets full of people who want to drink. "They tip more when it rains," Don says, and I figure he ought to know.

Janet teaches kindergarten at a nearby school. Their fridge is covered with pictures her students have drawn in class. Her own kids, she says, think they're too old to color. She gave me a picture once, a gray sky with green rain falling down on a house with no windows, a square red door. It's signed *Robby* and hangs just near the freezer handle.

When the dog left for good, I burned down its house in the backyard along with all the clothes Sarah left behind—jeans and sweaters and an L.L. Bean parka I bought with the Visa for Christmas. I spent five months paying it off, but when the dog left it was still snowing. No rain, just big white flakes that could turn to water or ice. I watched the house burn and threw whiskey on the flames, watching them rush bright and orange, sucking up all the air and making the snow melt. Don said later it was a crazy thing to do.

Sometimes I write her letters, long ones, and I imagine her reading them to herself out loud, her voice soft and pretty reading what I've said, the way it works sometimes with television. I always check the spelling.

Don's setting up cans on the stumps, and I'm finishing off my beer. I go out into the field, twenty yards or so, and say, "Hey, here's another."

Don turns and looks at me, and he looks funny. "Shit," he says, and I hear the gun, see him hit the dirt spread-eagled like one of his kids trying to make an angel in the snow, only backwards on the yellow grass.

"Get down!" he yells.

But I don't get down, I turn and hear two more shots, see the kid back there with a .22 automatic target pistol. A .22 has the longest and straightest trajectory because its rounds are so small. Also, it makes the most noise, and the kid's not even on the tarp. He's running around like Steve McQueen shooting at things. He ducks and rolls, fires. Does a somersault and lets off two more when he comes up, hair flying, the gun between his legs with two hands guiding. Now he leaps, the gun under one arm, and hits an empty oil quart thirty feet to Don's right. He's got to be aiming for something else, though probably only he knows what.

And I'm standing here in this field, watching this kid. Don's still yelling at me to get down and the kid is screaming *Pow!* and *Blam!* because the clip is empty.

"We have V.C. in the perimeter," he yells. "*Bamm!* I repeat, Victor Charlie is inside the wire. Request air support, ASAP."

Don's up now. The kid smiles, shrugs, says, "This is Bulldog," and starts to reach for a shotgun—but he stops. He stops and looks at Don, then me, and I'm wondering if I ever could have done anything that stupid. And I think probably I have, only I'm a lot older than the kid.

———————

"Hey," says the kid. "This is pretty much fun, you know?"

Don's not mad anymore. The tarp is scattered with shells from the automatics. I step back to the lawn chairs near the cooler and punch out my empties. I can't hit much today and my ears are ringing even with the earmuffs. I grab myself a beer and pass one each to Don and the kid. The kid says no thanks, he takes out his drugs. The sun feels hot. The beer is drenched with sweat, which means pretty soon the outside will be cooler than the inside, and the kid's shoulders are starting to turn pink.

We went to Florida once. I had a week coming. We were going to stay with cousins in St. Petersburg, what they call St. Pete, but Sarah was afraid of airplanes. She'd never been on one, she couldn't start now. We practiced some in the living room. I'd pretend I was the captain and tell her to look outside at all the big cities. "There's a big white cloud to your left," I'd say. "In case of emergency, be sure to breathe." Then I'd give her a Coke and ask if she wanted chicken or roast beef. I said it was a piece of cake. That millions did it every day. So when we finally left she said she was ready to try, but we weren't on the plane for more than five minutes when she started getting sick in a bag. We hadn't even moved, and then she started crying and saying, "Please? Please, Michael. Can we please just not do this?"

We left the plane but didn't get a refund; restrictions, they said. We ended up driving, from Connecticut to Florida. We only had three days in the sun this way, but Sarah still got burned and bought some aloe. I'd never even heard of aloe, and I kept telling her it was okay, on the way down in the car. For the way back, she brought tomatoes from her cousins' garden because I'd liked them so much, but once we hit Georgia, once she started driving, I began to throw them out the window. I'd take a bite out of each and throw them out the window one at a time at passing trucks.

I don't know—maybe that's what did it.

"Hey," I tell the kid. "You should get yourself some aloe."

We're all sitting down now, taking a break. My ears keep ringing and Don says to the kid, "Don't you know that stuff's illegal?"

"It doesn't matter," says the kid, wiping his nose. "My old man's a lawyer."

"I thought he drove a tank," Don says.

I'm not really listening anymore, but I hear, "Korea, the big one. Can I try out the .45?" He means the Colt automatic on the ground next to my Ruger.

Don says something, and the kid holds the gun in his hand, open so you can see it. He says, "My old man used to carry one of these."

"Yeah," says Don, nodding. "We had 'em in Vietnam, too."

The kid loads the clip with the butt of his hand. He checks the chamber, releases it. "What about you?" he says, looking at me. "What do you do?"

And I think, not much. I see what too much sun does. I wish he'd point the gun elsewhere because I know how things go, but I'm not sure this counts much anymore.

"Him?" says Don. "He cuts grass."

"Yeah," I say. "Usually I let it grow first."

G U N   L A W

A T   V E R M I L L I O N

Anna, 1988

Outside, on and across the lake, is snow. The snow shimmers inside a sheet of fragile ice, glazed now by a recently brief and nocturnal thaw. With ceremonial slowness my yellow lab walks across this ice—near-point, his fine head raised high in affected gentility.

"You stopped reading," says my father.

I withdraw and turn to face him, where he sits uncomfortably waiting for me to continue. He wears a weathered Stetson. Rings of dried sweat streak along the ridges of its snakeskin hatband. While doing an assignment in Santa Fe, I bought the hatband in an airport terminal; the carpet in the terminal was dull brown, I made the man at the counter put the skin in a box. For this year, I have given my father a bathrobe, plaid and Western, two breast pockets and two plastic mother-of-pearl eyes. These eyes stare out at me like his own from beneath the rim of his weathered hat.

"If you're tired," he says, "you don't have to keep reading." He shifts his weight and frowns heavily. "I am quite capable of reading all by myself."

The impatience in his voice makes me smile, and I am grateful for this span of lucidity: his hip hurts and he wants to know if Clay Orde and Johnny Buffalo can save Milly Ewell's mule packing business from Silver Jack Devaney. But I have stopped reading at a phrase where *guns cough heavy thunder*, because this coughing noise reminds me of the weather; I have stopped to look outside at the snow, now quiet, where my dog considers the ice, while in the kitchen nearby my mother brews a pot of her secret coffee—*it's the eggshells, you know*, her vowels long and drawn-out like the weather in Minnesota. I try to rediscover my place in my father's Western, I hear my mother call.

"Anna," says my father, no longer cross. "Go and help your mother."

And now his eyes harden with glaze, as if distorting his image of me into some amorphous nomenclature, Dutiful Daughter, as if I am devolving before his eyes like ice under a sky filled with sunlight and warmth, like snow.

The house accommodates my father's taste, only the kitchen belongs to my mother. From one wall hang small silver spoons, each bearing the name of place: Boston, Detroit, Kansas City. In the driveway stands a round gasoline tank, attached to which is a sign—*No Smoking*—in bold red print. On the back of my father's truck is a decal, an illustration of a horse—*Put Something Exciting Between Your Legs!* Over the fireplace hangs a mass-produced portrait of John Wayne, illustrating three separate moments of his mood and temperament. These things belong to my father, this is the language of his family, but in the kitchen my mother has her spoons.

From the porch, I call Duke inside. The air is painfully cold, biting through the fabric of my sweater, despite the sunlight, while Duke lopes like a horse, twin jets of steam spewing forth from his nose. Behind him is the long, frozen lake.

"Wipe his feet, Anna," says my mother.

I kneel to face my dog. His coat surprises me; it feels remarkably cold and I wonder how he can stay warm. I have grown unfamiliar with this weather, and until this visit Duke has never seen snow. Around his neck droops a red bandanna—a Western dog with Western habits, I explained. Between Duke's toes, the tufts are frozen with ice, and his hot breath makes him smell like a dog.

He leaves me and walks over to the running dishwasher, sniffing, lying down with his back to the gate where it's warm from the rinse cycle.

"I named him for Dad," I tell my mother.

She looks at me over a cup of coffee, her hands folded neatly, guiding the steam into shapes. I think I see her eyes wink, or wince, but I am not sure which.

After a while I pour my coffee, and my mother says, "Come. Sit with me."

We sit together and drink our coffee slowly.

———

As for my father's story, Silver Jack Devaney is responsible for the murder of Clay's foster parents and Milly's father, Jim. Milly is a nice girl, striking and feminine, but not necessarily pretty; she is the kind of girl my father admires—forthright, deferential, imaginative. She is the kind of girl my father made my mother want to be, the kind of girl I might have grown up to be had I not wanted to disappoint him. Clay is taciturn and lean; his boots add an extra three inches to his height and cause minor back-ache, which may account for his grim, unforgiving countenance. Clay is a man of the West, he is Nemesis made lean.

_____

When I drive my mother into Nisswa for shopping, she asks about Jim. I drive my father's truck because the snow is thick and steep, because the roads feel loose. I drive slowly and with the lights on and I wonder why it is I rarely feel comfortable driving.

"Jim's already dead," I say. "We open with Clay on the train."

My mother looks at me angrily. I watch the road, but feel her eyes just the same. Later, while we near the slotted parking on Main, I ask her if she wants me to wait. The snow has been stacked high around the parking meters: long, frozen faces.

"No," she says, "come with."

"In the midst of things," I explain, shutting off the engine. "A gentle knight was pricking on the plain. It's convention. What writers do. They start in the middle of things."

She looks at me and says, "We're very, very proud of you, Anna." She speaks to me absently, as if testing her voice to see if the words agree.

I put my arm around her shoulder, feel the wing of her blade sharp beneath her heavy overcoat. She is still too thin, weary, she will not wear the prosthesis. Instead, she fills herself with this visible, attenuating space.

"Mom," I say, "Jim moved back to Chicago."

My mother looks at me closely, her eyes vast and glassy; I watch her throat quiver and wish I had not told her this.

"Oh, Anna! Anna, why couldn't you have just married him?" She is shaking now, oblivious to the cold, sad more for my father than herself.

I worry about her health and try to make her warm.

Tonight I drive my car into Brainard, I go to the Last Turn Saloon. At the Last Turn the margaritas are spiked with hazelnuts. The floor is covered with sawdust, music spins from a reel-to-reel, I feel lonely and wish my parents had other children.

My father is a dude cowboy, was a dude cowboy while he was still limber enough to straddle his mare, Bay Lady. He boards her at a nearby summer camp off Round Lake. During the season he would assist with their riding program, teach camp counselors how to best teach kids. More often than not, he was in the way, but the kids loved him: they called him Slim, never knowing he knew more about insurance than he did horseflesh.

"Why visit now?" my father asked, in the living room propped with pillows. "What's so special about this Christmas?" He spoke to me hopefully, as if his time for a grandchild had finally come.

"No reason," I said. "I just wanted to see you and Mom."

And now his eyes dulled, he lost contact. "Milly's a fine woman. She's a fine woman, that one. She has a head like an Arabian."

I looked at my father and said, "Yes, she's a nice girl." I asked, "How is Mom?"

"Once we get this mess straightened out," he said, feigning gruffness, "I think we'll take a trip up to Carson City." He winked, told me to pass him the cigarettes on top of the mantel. Inside the fireplace sit an electric heating element and decorative flames which glow.

I opened the window, let the cold in to allow the smoke to leave. The sunlight streaked through the smoke and made it look more permanent than it might have been. He smoked in silence.

After putting the cigarette out in his coffee cup, he asked me to read from his book.

"Read the part about Moose Stokely," said my father. "That part always kills me."

When Jim left L.A. I knew I could not go with. I knew he would not return. It was as if we had reached a fork in our lives, a fork with only two tines—a tuning fork which when struck would resound with a shattering pitch when struck against something hard.

I helped my mother prepare dinner. She cooked lamb and potatoes while I chopped ingredients for salad. After all the years of training, she still will not trust me with anything crucial. My mother is very proud of her cooking.

When it was ready, she helped my father into his chair, wheeled him into the dining room and up to the table. While we ate I listened to the noise we made. I was cutting up my father's second portion of lamb, scraping away the mint jelly with my knife, when Duke began to scratch at the kitchen door.

"He wants to come in," I said, rising.

"It's too tough," my mother said, dropping her fork on the plate. "I left it in too long."

She rose, pushed the lamb from the platter into the white, lidded bowl of mashed potatoes. She took the bowl and left the room.

"Mom," I said, following, "it's fine. It's delicious. Please, Mom, don't throw it out."

"I'm not about to," she said, opening the door. She set the bowl out for Duke.

I tried not to do anything, I tried not to disappoint. "I'll pour the coffee," I said.

"You haven't finished yet. You haven't finished anything!"

"I'll pour the coffee, and you go back with Dad. Please?"

I waited for her to leave and went outside, took away the bowl from my dog. The food steamed in the cold and I set it on the railing of the porch. I took a handful of snow to wipe the grease from Duke's mouth. The snow made my hands cold, my skin melted the snow and turned my hands pink and numb; all the while I tried to wipe Duke's mouth, he lurched and squirmed, trying to break free. He finally knocked the dish from the railing. The bowl fell on a puddle of ice, cracked, the food spilling, my hands numb, the steam rising in the porch light while Duke nuzzled the lamb and potatoes.

I picked up the pieces of porcelain and tried to stack them in what remained of the bowl's shape; I pushed Duke away with my foot, wanting to kick him. When I looked up, I could see my mother in the kitchen window, watching, shaking her head slowly while I began to cry.

It was too cold to stay out long. Duke wanted to go in where it was warm and lie by the dishwasher, and I was afraid he would scratch the door or bark.

Across the bar is a table at which four men sit. The men appear relatively affluent; on vacation, perhaps. One wears a blue sweater over a yellow turtleneck, his face is bearded and long with sad eyes like Duke's. The man has caught my eye twice, and I have not yet avoided his. The walls are covered with streamers and some of the people wear paper party hats—small points of celebration rising up into the noise.

Sometimes I let my body feel the rhythm of the music from the reel-to-reel, I let myself feel loose amid the din of this saloon. Sometimes I try and look as if I do not mind really trying.

Moose Stokely owns the local watering hole. He used to be strong and tall, but now he has gone soft with the easy life of drink. Moose Stokely is the man who gave Johnny Buffalo a bottle of whiskey; it is he who made the Indian drunk. When Clay found out, he went to the bar and knocked some sense into Moose Stokely, told the once-strong man it was unfair to take advantage of a good Indian that way. Johnny Buffalo is Clay's right-hand man. The Indian is a good scout and faithful to Milly Ewell.

Later I take some clippings in to my father to show him what I do. They are mostly columns from the *Times*, an occasional feature. He looks at them but cannot focus on the print.

The sun streams through the window and makes the room bright, filling it with dust and clear, yellow light. My father holds up two fingers, which means he wants to smoke.

"No," I say. "Mom said you're not to smoke."

"It's a free country," my father says.

"I could read one to you," I say. "Here's one about fathers and daughters. Would you like me to read it?"

"Sheila," he says, "if I want a smoke, I'll goddamn have a smoke!"

"I'm Anna," I say. "I'm home visiting you and Mom. Mom's upstairs taking a nap."

He stares out the window and fidgets with his cast, drawing his fingers through the light, then underneath the plaster to scratch.

"Tell Anna," he says, "it's about time she had some goddamn children."

"First we have to read," I say, opening up his novel. I turn to the part where Silver Jack kidnaps Milly. Behind the barn,

Johnny Buffalo has already been bushwhacked, and for a while my father forgets who he is and why he is so angry.

———————

"Who are you?" says the man with the turtleneck.

I bite a part of small, twisted pretzel to convince myself I'm eating something, a bite just large enough to fill my mouth with salt. I lick the rim of my margarita and consider possibilities.

"I'm Milly," I say, after a while.

"Milly," he says, almost sadly. "That's a very pretty name."

———————

Inside the drugstore, my mother spoke with the pharmacist. She seemed to be on familiar terms with him, a small man with a shiny head and thick, plastic glasses. Because of my father's recurring bouts of incontinence, my mother visits frequently; normally, she has the neighbors' daughter drive her into town where here, at the Nisswa Store, she buys diapers for my father the same way she used to buy for me: one week's supply at a time, hoping never to purchase more than she will require. At any moment, one of us might outgrow our need.

"This is my daughter, Anna," my mother said to the pharmacist. "She's visiting her father from out West."

The druggist smiled as if he might have recognized me, he spoke easily: "Not the same Anna I used to know? That Anna was short and wore blue jeans!" He arched his eyes, shook his shoulders, and resumed pouring pale, summer-blue capsules into a large amber bottle. "You've turned into quite a woman," he said.

I think now it must be something he says often.

———————

"I live in Nisswa," I tell the man with the turtleneck. "I cocktail at Bar Harbor."

The man nods and considers my profession, he asks me if I'd like another margarita. His eyes are profoundly green—small pools of summer lake water, and I think Marguerite would have sounded equally pretty.

Early, very early before the pink of dawn, I walked across the frozen lake. The ice was thick beneath the snow. I could bury my boots beneath the snow and shuffle along on top of the ice. The ice did not feel especially slick.

I walked along the lake, avoiding the snowmobile tracks while Duke scampered around looking for something to chase, but there was nothing out but us: no birds, no loons, no peeping frogs. Everything was still and frozen as the sun.

After a while Duke tired of diving in the snow. He followed along beside me, sometimes rubbing up close against my leg. The bandanna around his neck provided a point of color, but as the sky brightened, the cloth was washed out with the light in the snow.

A minute or two before, the saloon quiets down: a young, pretty girl with long legs stands on a chair and looks at her watch, preparing herself and the rest of us for what is yet to come.

At midnight the horns begin, people scream and whistle their toys, paper hats fly into the air with confetti to mingle later with the sawdust. The room is a knot of bodies—a cluster of noise, varying in degree, feverish and uncertain.

I look at the man in the turtleneck standing beside me, politely shy. He looks at the others, at lovers and friends embracing, at the noise in the room as if studying its color. I put my arms around the man's soft shoulders and smell the soap in his beard, I have to reach for his mouth. It feels hot and makes me for a while stop reaching.

Clay's body aches with the long ride, but he feels that something is wrong back at the camp. He wants to push his horse the way he wants to push himself, but still his horse needs rest. After only one short hour of fitful rest, he wakes early in the desert, feeling deep in his long, taciturn bones the ache of something gone terribly wrong.

I drove home early, the lights of my car illuminating the moist roads slick with a fresh, calm and descending snow. The shape of the ruts seemed to melt with the flakes against the hot windshield, and I could smell the man with the turtleneck. The man said he was an investment broker and lived in Minneapolis. He asked me to come visit sometime soon.

When I pulled into the driveway, I turned off the engine to coast, the same way when I was younger I would make my boyfriends pull into the driveway so we could kiss before my parents knew I was home.

There was this one boy, Orion McClenahan, I used to love. He would visit with me during vacations, and we would go water-skiing or ride with my father at the camp. When we made love, we would keep the windows shut to keep mosquitoes from squeezing in. We would worry and sweat inside his Volkswagen and notice later that the glass had steamed thick with our heat.

Once, my father came out and saw us, in the car, beneath the frosted windows. I knew it was him because I could hear his boots, his stilted pace crunching the fine gravel of the driveway, and I know he said nothing because he knew if we did not do it here, we might do it elsewhere and upset my mother. Later he asked me if I and the boy I loved were really serious.

——————

I sat in my car until it grew cold and the windshield began to ice. As for Clay and Johnny Buffalo, they rode off after Silver Jack and Milly. Silver Jack was by now a desperate man. Johnny tracked through gullies and forks, led the men to water known only to Johnny. And the men pursued calmly, assuredly, knowing it was only a matter of time before Clay shot Silver Jack and rescued Milly, that striking young thing my father so admires. It was as if they had each read their own book, and in the end Clay is still tall and lean, only now he is also content.

——————

On Christmas morning, the first thing my father did was open the package with his bathrobe inside. He put it on and thanked his wife.

I gave her a spoon from Los Angeles and box of soap, which she said would be convenient. It was the same soap I use to clean my skin and make it healthy. I thought she would like it, but my parents have only each other, and I realized later that morning on the lake with my dog that this was *Gun Law at Vermillion*, that a body did what it had to and considered its consequence a matter of purpose—small, minor epics of hopefulness and deceit.

——————

Inside, beside the dry glow of the electric fireplace, sits my father. He has been watching me and Duke through the window, has watched me stop to wipe Duke's feet and remove my boots, my scarf, my long winter coat. My father wants me to have a boy, someone to grow up and be like him. The room is calm and quiet, bright with the still early sun. The light pours over the sill and bakes my father's hip.

"Good morning," I say, pleased that it is morning.

He fondles a cigarette, lights it with a match: one hand, thumb and forefinger together. I watch him think and study my face.

"How'd you finally make out with that dun?" he asks.

His voice is rough with smoke, and I feel the weight of his question, heavy like the fine powder of trail dust and disease. I walk across the room to sit at his side, wrap my arms around the long, white plaster of his cast.

"He's fine," I say. "He has gaits like butter."

I feel him listen, release a breath of smoke. "Yeah," he says, pausing to ruffle my hair, "but can he work with stock?"

The light feels warm, my father waits. He waits for me to get this just right.

"I want you to know," I say, starting slowly, "I've decided something very important."

"Duke's a fine name," says my father. "That's a damn fine name, Anna."

LOW FLYING

AIRCRAFT

At first he was found missing during a routine classified mission. Later, by way of a personal letter, Fennerstrom learned from a second lieutenant that it had been his brother's first trip; that he had jumped from a helicopter but never showed up for the lift home; that he still might be okay, he was only missing. Point being, it wasn't over with, and the odd thing, he thinks, is that there is simply no way to consider the experience without wishing it were really over with.

He came here in mid-term from a school in Jacksonville, Florida, which had suddenly gone defunct. This school, his new headmaster assured him, had money; Fennerstrom would be safe for the duration of his contract. To make the offer more attractive, the head volunteered an aquarium, "to add some color to your apartment—the boys really like fish."

When Fennerstrom asked what happened to the teacher he was replacing, the head scratched his elbow and smiled sadly. "He didn't get along with the gang very well. And he didn't like his apartment much."

The apartment, in Dorm B, consists of two modestly furnished rooms—a mattress and ten-gallon aquarium—off the upstairs hall, each loud and full of noise from the din of *Wake Up*, or *Treat*, which precedes *Activity*, or *Put to Sleep*. After *Put to Sleep*, after growing in need of relief, an older boy will rehearse a common practice: first a jolt, his leap out of bed, the echo of feet—fourteen stairs—*thump thump, thump* . . . the shrill squeak of hinge from one of the stalls below, the wooden thud of its door coming home. And then, later, following a swirl of surreptitious flush, the return to bed and maybe sleep. Sometimes at night, before he falls asleep, Fennerstrom thinks about the school nurse.

Each day for the past week has been his birthday. Peter Voyt, soon to graduate, started it. He will see Fennerstrom in the hall, on his way to class, or in the dining room waiting for grace, and say, "Happy birthday, Fenny," each time as if he has never before said this. Peter has only one eye and wears a patch. Smiling, his big eye rolling, Peter will begin to sing until everyone nearby catches on—sometimes up to sixty boys, singing "Happy Birthday" to Fennerstrom, the new Language and Social Studies teacher, and then Peter Voyt will stop. The boy will stand politely to the side while the others follow through with their rough and wandering pitch.

This morning at breakfast, Blane appears concerned. He passes Fennerstrom the thin, watered-down milk for his coffee and says, "Fenny, it looks as if you have a spot of pinkeye coming on."

"Allergies, Blane. Spring pollen."

"Oh. Yeah," he says, nodding. Blane is from Montpelier, nine years old and fat; he is allergic to sunlight. The school nurse, who also handles public relations and transportation, drives Blane into town for weekly shots.

"Blane," says Fennerstrom, "don't play with your butter."

"But I like butter," says Blane, beginning to whine.

"Pass the pancakes," says Stephen.

"Don't."

"Fenny," says Tommy Parga, "I gotta wink the twinkie!"

"Pass the pancakes," says Stephen.

"Ask me in ten minutes," says Fennerstrom.

"But I gotta bad!"

"Blane, I won't tell you again."

"Please?"

"Fenny," says Stephen, "can I please have some pancakes?"

Fennerstrom stirs his coffee, watches it turn a dull, muddy brown. He gestures with his thumb, indicating permission for Tommy Parga to leave the table, and he tells Blane to pass the pancakes.

"Jeezum!" says Ben Wilmington-Roch, throwing down his fork.

Fennerstrom watches the swirls inside his cup, and he hears Ben's voice, distantly, as if it is wandering far away.

"Take your meds," he hears himself say, "and you can go too."

———————

Brian Metcalf is president of Student Council, as well as the school bully; during *Showers*, he pisses on the younger kids.

"Fenny," he says, in a small classroom cramped with fifteen-year-olds, "you know what I don't understand?"

"Does it have to do with tense?"

"What I don't understand is if you're such a liberal, commy kind of guy, what are you doing here teaching the kids of millionaires?"

"My parents aren't millionaires," says Peter Voyt.

"Mine are," says Ben Wilmington-Roch.

"Brian," says Fennerstrom, thinking that if you reverse the vowels you'll get *Brain*, "what is the past tense of lie?"

"No," says Ben Wilmington-Roch. "Mine really are."

"Which one?" says Brian Metcalf. "I mean, what kind of lying are we talking about here?"

He thinks the boys are like cubs, the way they giggle and fart, curl up with one another while he tells them stories. The way they fight. This afternoon Donald bit Bob Kindig's ear, and Bob Kindig punched Donald in the nuts.

"Twice!" says Donald, pointing. "Twice, right there!"

The tone of injustice causes Fennerstrom to smile, he recalls a time when he fought with his brother—on a beach near which they were raised. They were raised by affluent and understanding parents; they lived amid a polyglot of culture where everyone was healthy and tan. Later, when he left for the mainland, when he began to protest the war actively, Oahu was how he pictured Vietnam might be if it too were full of tourists and hotels.

His brother was his twin. They were born on the same day, they wore the same clothes. Each liked to surf. Their room was always full of trophies covered with fine island dust. Together they would sit on the shore and watch the waves, the patterns of sets: seven to each like days or long, slowly passing nights.

Tonight, now during *Put to Sleep*, after Donald and Bob Kindig have made up, he tells the boys a story about two buffalos who went to Asia in order to teach people how much fun it was to be a buffalo, with horns and big, furry humps, until they realized Asia had its own buffalos, water buffalos, and so the two buffalos went home and almost got skinned.

"Why?" Bob asks, rubbing his ear.

"Because," Fennerstrom says, softly, "they were too sensitive."

"Why were they so sensitive?" Donald asks. "I mean, I thought buffalos were dumb? I thought—"

"No, but they are very, very sensitive. And when you're burly and sensitive, it's easier to fight with Indians than be friendly."

"Oh," says Donald. "S'pose, s'pose they might have died, huh?"

"Yes," he whispers. "Or worse. They could have been turned into nickels. Or tipis, with pictures of themselves drawn all over the outside."

"Oh man," says Bob Kindig.

"Oh man," says Donald. "Tough."

To this date, the fourteenth of May, 1976, Fennerstrom has never spoken with the school nurse, and spring has finally come north. Fennerstrom has watched it evolve slowly, has watched the winter devolve: two contradictory motions, each full of promise—like the playing fields, thick now and overgrown. The boys are keeping watch for the first thunderstorm, and Fennerstrom feels himself growing older. This world turning green tires him, makes him feel dull and fatigued. During *Activity*, which today was an *All Student* and *New Faculty* soccer match, they were visited by a squadron of transports—dull green transport planes flying routine missions under the border. The boys stopped to watch, to wave to the pilots, to the men flying these vast planes floating slowly and low over the trees, these dull green machines which weighed more than most things on earth. It gave Fennerstrom time to catch his breath.

Now while he shaves, during *Showers*, Fennerstrom listens

for rain; he leaves open his door—a public display of availability. He smooths the soap into his beard, grips the razor carefully when he hears a small, timid voice.

By the sound, the pitch and cadence, Fennerstrom knows it is Stephen. When Stephen smiles, he squints, as if happiness affected the quality of his vision. He wears a wool coat and one of his father's loud, fashionably wide ties. The tip nearly brushes the boy's knee.

"What'cha doing?"

"Shaving."

"Oh."

The boy watches Fennerstrom closely, as if double-checking. "You look funny," he says, smiling.

"Here," says Fennerstrom. He squirts soap into Stephen's hand. "You better start practicing."

He shows Stephen what parts to cover, finds him an old razor with no blade. "You have to be careful now," he says. "If you sneeze, you just might slice your nose off."

"Like your thumb," Stephen says, looking.

"Like my thumb."

The boy stands on top of an upside-down wastebasket and wipes soap from his nose. "I won't sneeze."

After finishing one side, his cheek flushed and wet, Stephen says, "Wow, this stuff tingles!"

"That means your whiskers are growing."

"Whiskers," says Stephen, practicing. "Whiskers. Cats have whiskers."

His eyes are thin, happy slits.

Supper is clam chowder, salad, old bread with apple butter, and the boys are visibly sad. They are too young to appreciate clams or apple butter, both of which Tommy Parga describes in vivid, scatological detail. Fennerstrom shifts the swell of their conversation, listens to himself explaining the origins of the phrase *happy as a clam* to Ben Wilmington-Roch and Blane, wondering if either listens, when the sky lights up with a tremendous electrical flash.

Silence falls, the boys stare out the wide windows. The atmosphere is still, black, full of inexplicable wonder. When the noise finally arrives—thunder—the kids cheer.

Howard the Genius begins to describe Ben Franklin and his experiments, and one of the boys at Fennerstrom's table, he's not sure who, says, "Not now!" Howard looks hurt, his bright eyes turn down; his parents are vegetarians, and he is not permitted to eat clams. Fennerstrom spoons his soup, telling himself, "High tide. At high tide, the clams are happy because they're safe."

He's wondering how he can work this into a lesson on geography, how it might be connected with the pull of the moon or the danger of a tide which rolls excessively low, when he realizes he's listening to the weather and absolutely nothing else.

———————

Fennerstrom has not been laid in six months, a fact which recently concerns him—as if perhaps he is growing too old for, or aware of, or uncomfortable with the rites of intercourse. Here he feels himself cloistered, shut off from everything outside himself. What troubles him most, though, is why he is not more concerned. He thinks it was the same in Jacksonville and, before that, Carbondale.

"Fennerstrom," says Brian Metcalf, in the hall between periods, "I know when your birthday is. And you had better watch out."

"Watch out?" He has drunk too much beer the night before, sitting up late in one of his rooms, listening to Paul Simon, watching his fish and drinking warm beer. His refrigerator has stopped working. The cans are hidden safely inside a file cabinet he picked up during a trip to Boston, but he worries now about his breath—still stale. His head feels thick and slow.

"Yeah," says Ben Wilmington-Roch. "The whole school knows. We checked the office. Jennifer's going to bake you a cake, even."

"Who's Jennifer?"

"The nurse!"

"Oh," Fennerstrom says. "I thought she was called The Nurse."

Peter Voyt enters the hall, whistling, practicing a walk he is trying to master for the Spring Festival skit; it appears to be a cross between John Wayne and Elvis Presley. When he sees Fennerstrom and Brian Metcalf and Ben Wilmington-Roch, Peter Voyt starts off the song: "Happy birthday very soon, Happy birthday very soon . . ."

His wide, collusive smile seems unavoidably close, and its presence adds to the ache already growing behind Fennerstrom's eyes.

————————

Most of the boys are from New England. The big joke among the older faculty is to ask Bobby Boyle what state he lives in. Nine times out of ten, Bobby Boyle will say, "Brattleboro."

Today on his morning off Fennerstrom drives into Brattleboro to deposit his check and shop for his birthday. He wants a new copy of Kerouac's *On the Road*, and he plans to buy for his car either an eight-track or cassette player, whichever is cheaper, and maybe some tapes. Afterwards he will return to Westminster by way of the highway because he will have spent too long dawdling in town, and he will drive his car fast while the miles click over and over and over. He'll pass a roadway sign—LOW FLYING AIRCRAFT—and when he finally pulls into the long, rutted drive of the school, he'll have just enough time to fix a cup of instant coffee, sneak a cigarette, enough time to read his horoscope in *The Reformer* before going off to *Badgers, Writing Group B.*

———————

After lunch is *Surprise,* which means cake. The hall is noisy and raucous—the kids eager for a celebratory boost of sugar. Peter Voyt has secured permission from the head to preside over the official singing. He rings the buzzer, waits for quiet, and looks to Fennerstrom.

"Today as we know is the infamous Mr. Fenny's birthday! So," he says, waving his long, growing arms, "without further stuff—"

The room fills loud, full of voice and earnest effort, while Kurt the Snot Blower brings out cake and Ben Wilmington-Roch punches Tommy Parga in the arm, while Blane looks at Fennerstrom and smiles widely.

———————

This morning he received a birthday card; inside it was signed *Happy Birthday, Jennifer,* and now just a few hours later he has more visible proof: his apartment is cluttered with blue and green streamers, scotch tape, and signs. His empty beer bottles have been removed from the filing cabinet and filled with water; they sit in various spots on the floor like bowling pins, each waiting to be struck. His cigarettes are strewn along his bed, his packages fit neatly inside the aquarium, and two of the fish are dead. They float slowly near the top.

Along one wall hangs a long sign, autographed by each of the boys, drawn on with crayon and nontoxic markers, wishing him a happy birthday. Beneath the larger message, he recognizes the small, twisted scrawl of Bob Kindig: *Pleez bot lev!*

———————

Seven years ago today his twin brother stood nearby on the beach with an Emergency First Aid kit while Fennerstrom steadied his own hand over a coconut, while he waited for a wave to wash in before severing his thumb and forefinger with a machete. His brother used gauze and tape to slow the blood before driving him off to the hospital. Fennerstrom had meant only to take the thumb, and his brother swore he'd go to Canada first. But his brother didn't go to Canada, and the blood had washed pink with the thin milk of coconuts.

———————

At The Common Place Restaurant, the women wear gossamer and batik; the men, tie-dye and jeans. It is a hirsute community, Fennerstrom thinks, where neither men nor women shave. He wonders how these people make a living. Meanwhile the tables have been cleared away, the patrons have all donated their money into the *Common Bowl* and now wait patiently for a band from Kenya to finish setting up. Beneath a door drifts a faint, friendly vapor of hash, and he sees many people he thinks he might have known, at one time or another, were they some place else. But here he is content to lean, to gaze through the crowd, back to wall and haunches tight in a squat; he works on a Rolling Rock longneck and wonders if his brother would like this place. He rises, feeling his muscles stretch, and steps inside the restroom to smoke a joint.

Inside the light is dim. He turns and recalls the way his brother's yellow hair blows in the breeze, lighted like small, lightly spun threads; he sees the hair, against the blue sky and rising water. The two of them walk the shore of Kailua Beach, each like the other—seventeen, he thinks. Up ahead lie two black-haired girls, tops loose, their brown backs to the sun, and his brother says, "Which do you want?"

"Both," he says. "I want both."

The image recedes with the sound of their laughter, the sound of someone banging outside to come in. Meanwhile Fennerstrom waits, he watches the open window while the window pulls the smoke outside and lifts it up into the air.

———————

The music is loud, tribal and percussive—the room filled with the swaying of solitary dancers, men and women alike, dancing inside a space which smells like sweat and bottled beer. The wooden floor rolls beneath the bodies and the music beats, beats on—ritualistic, formative, shaping the space of the dance with its ineluctably precise rhythms. He feels the rhythm of a woman nearby, watches the way her bare feet straddle the floor, the way her hips catch her balance while she draws near, barely, a half foot or so where she again plants her feet, firmly, rooted in oak to support the swelling dance. The legs beneath her skirt meet somewhere near the hips, and he feels himself drawing nearer, close enough to smell the flavor of her soap, strikingly familiar like plumerias and salt. He thinks about the smell of salt and some place far away from where he is, and he feels himself alone. Here, in this crowd dancing with the woman nearby. Here, where he lets himself go, hoping now never to return unless he too is not with someone else.

THE RANGE

OF MONOCULAR

VISION

Peter, 1986

I

I don't remember how I used to see, before I lost the vision in my left eye, but sometimes I dream in perspective. This only when I sleep, or remember things. Normally I see the color of shapes, and I like to keep my hands close to the things around me—Helen, and the things we've tried to do with our lives.

The dress Granny bought was nice: a rich flannel reminiscent of Monet, pastels and lilies with a high collar and white lace. When Helen put it on, with the door open and windows wide, she looked as if she'd suddenly been placed into the nineteenth century. Only her hair altered the scheme, short black hair tucked under the collar, her lean, muscled torso just be-

68

neath. The best way to acquire muscles, she'd say, was to want them.

"Do you think Bob will buy me a suit?" I asked.

"I will if he won't," she said, not listening. She admired herself in the light, twirling. She asked if I really liked it.

"Yes," I said. "I like it."

"You know," she said, "it could be a wedding dress."

"Granny would prefer white."

"But it could be, couldn't it?"

"Yes," I said. "It could be."

She turned to me and pulled the dress over her head—an easy, lucid gesture. She put her hand on the flat of her stomach and said, "How do I look now?"

I stood there a while, taking her in, and she walked to the window. She looked outside at the late summer lawn. The window was framed in oak, and after a while she put both hands on her stomach. She leaned into the sill with her hands, she crossed an ankle, and she stood there all by herself, balancing.

II

We left most of Helen's things with her grandparents in Chicago. We drove her father's truck to Nashville and moved me into an apartment I'd rented on West End. The place was close to campus, a hamburger joint and laundromat—Vandyland—and the building itself made me feel as if I would be living once again in Tennessee. Its floors were wood, walnut trim along the walls, mahogany doors with panes of lead glass which had settled like an aging body—thicker now at the bottom than the top. The ceilings were high and plaster, the plumbing deficient. I had a sun room with a ceiling fan and orange paint inspired by a former tenant. The sun room looked out across West End to an automatic bank teller, and I had no furniture.

Outside it rained. I unpacked my pots, setting them on their cardboard boxes, listening to the weather while Helen hung my clothes in the bedroom closet.

When she came into the living room, Helen seemed eager about furnishing my new apartment: she could pick out my sofa the way she did my sweaters. "We should all go shopping together," she said, sitting down on the floor to call Betsy and Miles.

She picked up an old phone that had been left behind and listened. "It doesn't work yet," she said.

"It's not going to."

"What do you mean?"

"I mean it's not worth it."

"Well what are you going to do, write?"

"You can call me at the studio, if you want."

She didn't say anything, which is what I'd hoped for. I wanted her to see what we were buying into: her in Chicago, me in Nashville.

She shrugged. "Well it's your life," she said, standing. "I'm going to go find a phone."

Three years ago, after Helen took third at state for the 200-meter medley, we were released into the world with good intentions and a baccalaureate. Helen and I loaded up our life for Boulder, Miles started writing songs, and Betsy began to play with the Nashville Symphony. Once Betsy explained to me why she became a musician. "My mom made me practice," she said. "It's as if it were one big accident."

Now she was running ahead of Miles across a J.C. Penney parking lot. "Peter!" she screamed. "Peter the Potter!"

She leaped, her legs and arms all around me and big sloppy kisses. We all said hello and wondered what was different about us now. It was still drizzling, overcast and damp on a gray parking lot with few cars. We had arrived early, and I realized that Miles had put on weight, that Helen's hair was shorter, that

Betsy looked the same: short and stubby with long wavy hair swimming down her back. I had shaved my beard.

We sat on the curb in the drizzle drinking coffee and waiting for the store to open. We listened to Betsy talk about their upcoming move to Phoenix. "We're going to join a Salsa band," she explained. "Guac N' Beans!"

"Really," Miles said. "Betsy used to know the drummer."

"I'll bet she did," said Helen.

Miles lit a cigarette and asked what we were doing here.

"To pick out Peter's furniture," Helen said.

But I said no, that I was just looking for a mattress—something cheap to sleep on, and it all seemed more awkward than it should have been. I kept thinking maybe we could have stood more rehearsal, which is what usually happens when people get married. They rehearse.

The wedding was set for Sunday, and that night Miles and I went out by ourselves so Betsy and Helen could talk about us the way we wanted to talk about them. We went to a bar where Miles had been doing gigs—"Free beer," he said—where we played pool and I watched local women with sophisticated accents. I told him about my shows, about my pseudo-patron in Denver and my new slot at the university.

"Sure," he said, "but how about you and Helen?"

"We're fine, really. We do what we want."

"What do you want?"

"I don't know," I said, lining up a shot, stopping. I told him I only knew what I didn't want. "Never be afraid to take the duck," I said, and I brushed the Nine into the side.

Miles lit a cigarette and watched me circle the table. He trimmed the ash with his cue and said, "We're not really getting married, you know. I mean, we're having the ceremony and all, but there are no papers. We don't want the paperwork. It's easier this way. We're free to screw up."

I listened, but not very carefully. He explained the rationale while I concentrated on the game. Pool is a sport even a guy with one eye can play well. When I was ready to draw on the Eight, I looked up at him and smiled.

"Jesus," he said. "Don't you ever stop?"

But I didn't stop. I kept winning, Miles kept talking, and that night when I walked home I thought about the way things were three years ago when I had once thought things would never change. That I would become famous and live in Boulder for the rest of my life. That Helen and I would grow old like Granny and Bob and teach our kids to ski. That 1983, somehow, had meant everything was set, only now everything was different and I was walking home along West End telling myself I was back in Tennessee.

"Tennessee," I told myself. "Tennessee."

Helen was up waiting. She had slid the mattress into the dining room beneath the open bay windows; wind and light poured in from the street on her and an old cotton quilt my mother had made while she was pregnant with me. Helen sat in her green pajamas with feet, drinking wine on the new mattress, my mother's blue and white quilt wrapped around her shoulders.

"Hi!" she said.

"Hi," I said. "Who's this woman in my house?"

"I like your house," she said. "But I think you need a couch."

I kissed her and changed into my sweats while she watched. I went into the kitchen and she said, "We could go get you a couch. Tomorrow. We could get a nice big one with a hide-a-way bed for your bimbos!"

"What bimbos?" I said, returning.

"You know what bimbos. All those bimbos." She swept her hands through the air, a little late, and took a breath. "That way, when I came to visit, you could hide all your bimbos in the couch."

"I don't want a couch," I said.

"Sure," she said, nodding. "We'll get you a bimbo couch!"

I climbed into bed and pulled the blanket over us. She asked what Miles and I had talked about.

"Not much. We talked about Phoenix. About Betsy."

"About me?" she asked, hopefully.

"Yes, about you."

And then she started crying, her head on my shoulder and crying, her voice rusty and weak. I put my arm around her and pulled her closer, reached over with the other for my water to give her some. Now she sat up and knocked the water from my hand, the jar spinning across the wooden floor. She threw off the blanket and looked at the jar, at me, looking me hard in the face and squinting one eye so she could see me the way I always saw her.

"Just one thing I want to know," she said.

"We know too much already," I said, reaching for the quilt. "Let's sleep."

"No," she said, pulling away the quilt.

"Sleep."

"No. I want to know now!"

"Look," I said. "It just happened. It wasn't your fault."

She was swinging at me now. I caught her wrists while she kept swinging, crying, while she began to think what we were beginning to understand.

"Well it wasn't yours!" she screamed. "It sure as hell wasn't goddamned yours!"

And then I let her go, I let her hit me until she tired. After a while she finally stopped and I felt better about things, and when I tried to sleep I thought about how good it had felt, her hitting me like that—her hands finding direction, bunched into small fists like apples while she kept pounding at my back.

III

Allen Hardwick, a mutual friend, had agreed to perform the service. Allen had finished with our class; he was later expelled from seminary for plagiarizing a paper on Augustine's *Confessions*. Because Miles and Betsy wanted to leave for Phoenix directly following the service, Allen had arranged with his aunt to host a reception, the day before the wedding, at her place—a large, complex home not unlike Granny and Bob's, complete with tall trees and a swimming pool. Allen's aunt was a Lifetime Friend of the Nashville Symphony and former cellist.

I took my gift, a pot I had made for Helen. I stood in the aunt's den which overlooked the backyard and pool, and Allen said, "It's very nice, Peter Voyt. You could put a good many things inside a pot like that."

The pot sat tall, bell-like and blue with an elliptical lid; atop the lid to serve as a handle stood a ring, a large ring which had occasioned the idea for the pot. "It's a wedding pot," I said, pointing. "I made it for Betsy and Miles."

Allen placed it on a table and began to explain the role of theocracy in an informational age. Outside, the day was bright and simple—full of nice breezes and rich grass, the kind of grass which won't grow in Colorado. The sky felt profoundly blue, and I listened to Allen talk, the soft, easy rolling of his vowels, wondering what it was they meant. I watched people outside wander beneath the sky with drinks: pretty young people with pleasant voices and strong bodies amid sentimental music from the seventies.

Out on the deck of the pool lay Helen, reaching occasionally to sip from a glass of diet soda. She wore a trim red bikini she'd bought in Saint-Tropez—her Sunday suit, she called it. She talked with Miles, who wore a gray T-shirt and gray trunks. Betsy wore a coral-blue one-piece, high on her hips, stretching her short legs and making them seem as long as her hair. She bounced on the tip of the diving board and announced she would perform a one-and-a-half, which she did, her hair following the curve of her body—belatedly, like sound which travels a long distance in waves. People applauded.

I excused myself from Allen and went out to the pool. I stripped to my shorts. I sat on the steps and watched Betsy run inside the house, dripping and laughing. She returned a few minutes later and plunged into the far side of the pool near Miles and Helen. I listened to music blasting from the bar and watched Betsy swim the length of the pool underwater.

"It's great!" she said, scrambling up the steps. "It's a great pot, Peter. I love it!" She kissed my cheek. She felt cold and wet.

"What the hell did you say?"

"What?"

"To Helen. What did you tell her?"

She sat beside me on the deck, reaching into the water to splash her face. The water dripped down her neck and beaded on her chest. "I just told her what I felt, that's all." She turned to study my face. "Because I wanted to, Peter. Don't get mad just because that's how I feel. I'm sorry it's over."

"You told her that?"

"Of course I told her that. I told her everything."

"What about Miles? What are you doing with Miles?"

She looked toward Helen and Miles, across the pool where Miles smoked a cigarette and watched the sky. "Miles is safest," she said. "He's not like us. He can only love one thing at a time."

"And what makes you think I can't?"

She laughed deeply and tossed her hair. "I just wanted her to know. That's all."

I felt the water pulling at my legs, gently, and I could smell her hair. I watched Helen sit up, her back straight while she fixed her top—eyes closed, her hands tucked up behind her back.

"God," Betsy said, "she's beautiful."

"She's going back to Chicago."

"I know. I'm sorry, Peter. I really am."

"It's different," I said, thinking it was. "It's different this time."

"Peter," she said, rising, "come swimming. Come swimming and give me your shorts!"

I reached up and pushed her in the pool. I sat on the deck and watched Betsy swim through the water. In 1981, over in Knoxville, I had watched Helen nearly win the 100-meter breast-stroke. Instead she placed second, and we began dating once the season was over. Now, years later, I watched the way the light shimmered inside the waves of this pool. Like electricity, one line connecting with another and another until the whole span of water was tied together in knots.

IV

Last night we lit candles to kill the glare. We drank wine from coffee cups and listened to music on the box with auto-reverse. The box sat in the corner and the music echoed off the plaster walls. We sat on the hard floors among plants Betsy and Miles had given me. "Housewarming plants," Betsy had said. "So your house feels warm." We sat on the floor among my housewarm-ing plants and said things about ourselves, we took pictures in the empty rooms, we drank wine until we grew sleepy and fell asleep together—our limbs tangled like pups. And I remem-ber, while nodding off to sleep, my head nodding in the crotch of Betsy's arm, I remember dreaming what it was we all knew together that none of us knew alone, and I thought it must be a kind of knowledge that's bigger than yourself—a kind that's truly frightening if you're not with those you really think you know. I thought about Helen swimming in a pool, one lap after another until each was all the same and it was no longer a matter of losing count.

In the morning, Betsy and Miles would be married in six hours. While they left, Helen and I sat on the floor watching the door open and close.

The room fell suddenly still. I leaned on one elbow and looked across the floor at Helen: legs long, arms stretched out behind. Her body looked like clay, like a body which would only move when you wanted it to, and she looked at the ceiling and breathed slowly. We both know we're on the edge of something irrevocable and sharp, and I watched the shape of her face. I watched her rise and leave for the shower. Later I followed her in and together we took a long cool shower. Afterwards we sat in the sun room. We sat on the floor under my mother's quilt drinking hot coffee from my water jar watching the light.

Now my new plants stretch in the light, and Helen's dressing. She's in the next room combing her hair, puffs of powder under her arms like chalk, and I think maybe things would be different if we'd had a kid. Spontaneous abortion is what the doctor called it, and maybe all we need is a good look at the shape of things to come, of possibility. Maybe we just need a little space.

V

This is the wedding: Sunday afternoon, people in nice clothes. Friends, mostly. Helen on the right, behind Miles. I'm behind Betsy. I keep the ring in my pocket where it belongs.

We pose on the lawn of a large antebellum home. The wide swimming pool was a later addition, like the tennis courts and sauna. Betsy wears a cornflower blue dress, and Helen wears her Monet. Miles and I both stand in suits: mine is gray, the same one my father bought me when I went off to college on scholarships and financial aid for the handicapped. I am, after all, legally blind.

Allen wears a tuxedo. The short white collar sits high, neatly clipped. "Miles Davenport," he says, "are you going to wed this person?"

"Yes."

"What?"

"Yes, I'm going to wed this person."

"And you, Betsy O'Gush. Are you going to wed this person?"

"Yes, Allen. I'm going to wed this person."

Allen smiles and looks important. He says, "You all are free now to recite your vows."

I take the ring from my pocket and give it to Betsy. The ring feels smooth and heavy, full of air. Betsy takes the ring while Miles says something about wanting to be her friend, lover, companion: this is the kind of vow they take, and it seems to me sensible. They make no part for death. When my mother married my father, she was still a virgin and Catholic. I look at Helen and think she'd be a good mother. If we had kids, they'd be pretty and smart like us, the best people.

After Betsy kisses the groom, Miles turns to us. We all clap and shout, and Miles points at Betsy and says, "This is my wife. This is my beautiful wife!"

Helen kisses them both. She kisses Allen and I'm watching Allen's aunt. She stands in back behind all the guests, and she watches the wedding party as if she, too, is unsure of our application.

"Peter," says Betsy. We stand near the pool where the party has scattered with champagne and rice while guests swim in the water. Some guy wearing jeans and a tweed coat lands in the pool; I think I used to know him and feel the spray of the pool while Betsy and I kiss again, her mouth cool with champagne as she puts something in my hand. Warm cotton.

"I don't have a garter," she says.

I lost my eye in a freak accident. I used to tell people how it happened, but nobody believed me.

"You have a lovely home," I tell Allen's aunt. "It's very big."

"Thank you," she says, looking at my eye.

I was nine when it happened. I was outside on a porch. There were hummingbirds nearby. Hummingbirds with long, narrow beaks. No one ever believes it.

"I especially like the tennis courts. Clay. It really is amazing what they're doing now with clay."

"Yes," she says, "clay really is best, unless one is training for Wimbledon, of course."

"It was an accident," I say, pointing.

"Yes," she says. "Of course."

I don't play tennis, but I love everything that's beautiful. I love leaves and misery and the feel of swollen skin. And I think it's easier to love Helen knowing we aren't going to make it, as if somehow this failure exonerates us, me, her—twisting the shape of our past into knots like one of Van Gogh's olive trees.

One eye, one ear—Van Gogh and I really have a lot in common. I stand out front on the driveway drinking my wine. Helen's making a sign to place on the trunk of Miles' car. She uses Liquid Embroidery, a thick indelible paint from a tube. She's on her knees, working the tube, the red paint squeezing slowly onto the posterboard near a bottle of champagne. She's stuck on the second half of a heart.

"I love hearts," I say.

She stops, shakes the tube. "It's stuck," she say. "The paint won't go."

She sets the tube on the cement and stands to stretch her back—a fluid, graceful arch. Far away a church bell rings, long peals ringing through the air. I look at the tube of paint, at the sign, at the tube of paint. When you have only one eye, things always look closer than they seem, and I wonder what will happen if I step on it, or if she really knows who she's talking to.

"You try," she says.

"What?"

"Go on, you try."

I remember the curve of her back, the small part where it starts, I look at the paint and try. My foot comes down hard on the tube and blows off the seal, the car is spattered in red like the sign and cement and tree behind her. Helen's Monet appears to bleed, and she just stares at me, her mouth caught, the black-rose of her lips still and open.

THE FUTURE

OF RUTH

It seemed to her the house was a flame, dazzling in the heat of the sun with its center hot, edges trim and undeniably blue like cornflowers. Orion sometimes wore blue, he'd said, because it matched his eyes; she preferred black. Her eyes were absent of any real color, were more likely the shade of some color wanting relief—a shadow of something vigorous and more bright.

"Miss Eva's," Orion said as they approached, hand in hand against the traffic.

And she felt as if this house had somehow stood firm, as if it had purposely repelled traffic and prefabricated housing by way of its circumspect indifference, its smell of heat.

"That's where Miss Eva lives," he said, squeezing.

Ruth could feel her hand slip in their sweat. She felt the throb

of his fingers, the recurrent stares latching onto them from behind a maze of oncoming automobiles: a mildly syncopated
rhythm which came and passed on and came again. Orion, in
long khaki shorts, a washed-out rugby shirt, sleeves rolled, his
limbs tan and villous. Here people would not be gazing at him,
but at the two of them together in front of this house which
beckoned each hither, into the offices of Miss Eva and her eyes
which would, purportedly, leaf among the documents of your
soul, or your heart. Your palms.

"I don't want to, Orion."

"Really Ruth. It'll be good."

"She's probably just a sham. Why waste it?"

"A sham's not a waste. It's a sham." He laughed, set his hand
along the ridge of her neck and kissed her ear. "You taste like
salt," he said.

And you, she thought, smell like me. She worried that Eva
might recognize it, wondered why this worried her—why it
might even matter.

Because she shouldn't see anything beforehand, Ruth thought.
Because a palmist was paid to read wrinkles, not earrings or
shoes. She had removed her jewelry before leaving the house,
had purposely worn a white top—cotton and backless, but white
nonetheless—red shorts and bleached sneakers. She soothed her
bloodshot eyes with expensive sunglasses; the only brand, as
near as she could tell, one might actually see upon her body.

Orion always wore suspenders. Like her, he didn't work. He
bought occasional groceries and lived with her in a small room
with plywood floors, windows for walls which looked out over
displaced palm trees, bottle trees, bougainvillia and squash;
where they shared a house with three men, two of their lovers
and a dog. And she had let Orion into the space of her room, had
found a place for his hiking boots inside a milk crate. He wore
them now, beneath his long khaki shorts, the laces green and
almost loose.

"I'm on the move," he'd said. "Anything that doesn't fit in that pile goes." He sold off his darkroom equipment, and she watched him compress with the precision of a vice his underwear and aloha shirts, a Spanish-American dictionary of slang into his backpack. She watched him discard the things of his life: a clock radio, a blender, paperbacks which had sat gathering dust and mold on dirty wooden shelves. He was setting himself free, flinging himself upon the world outside of his wealthy family with lingering Midwestern habits. He was going to look for something, on the prowl. "The great hunter," he said. "Only I don't need a belt."

Below her bed sat the milk crate, his cameras and backpack, a dry wooden chair ready to split, and her books. The bed hung from her ceiling in lengths of galvanized chain, and it was from this spot, slightly swaying, that afterwards they would read Goethe to each other or drink wine, where they would look out into the yard and watch for mosquitoes.

"I'm going to Peru," he had said. "In Peru you can buy a gram of coke for ten dollars."

"Do you mind if I smoke?" she said.

And later, with the smoke clouding the light gray, he took her picture.

She once knew a man who had driven his car off a cliff. Mr. Fennerstrom had taught her history, and she knew her life-line was short. Her mind was strong; her past, fixed and spent. Her intuition intersected her heart, briefly, like a breath of wind. These things she knew certain as the back of her hand, with her thin blue veins swimming just beneath the skin of her wrist.

He should stop wanting to know and do it, she thought. He

should pack up and go, take his boots and walk away the way he planned, the way she kept planning for it. To linger was to go slowly, and to go slowly worked only with sex: with the chains swaying and their bodies riding one another until neither could be sure of anything but their own insoluble heat, slick with sweat like the space now between their hands. She wanted to leave this porch. She wanted to go home and ascend her bed and hover over the things in her room until he decided something. If they just went home now, maybe something would work its way open, naturally, like the foreskin on a blister ready to heal.

Orion was speaking. "Are you Eva?"

The woman said she was. She wore black hair, oily and wet with a streak of silver. Her face sat heavily among folds of yellow skin, and her eyes seemed painfully black.

"You want reading? Ten dollars, read. Twenty for tarot."

"How long's a reading?" Orion asked.

"I do past, present, future. I do love and success. I do anything you want." Eva stopped, looked at Ruth. "You too," Eva said. "Yes, you too. Come in, please."

"You go first," Orion whispered.

"No," she said, changing her mind. "No, I'll go."

Inside, the house smelled like an old woman. They sat in a room with a high plaster ceiling and a fan swirling slowly above her—the blades and their shadows. She let Eva take her hands, set them face up on a vinyl ottoman littered with old issues of *National Geographic*. She watched the old woman settle on the floor, cross-legged and imminent. Orion sat nearby on a brown couch.

"Now," Eva began, "what I say is what I see. I tell you good things, I tell you bad, but you cannot get mad at me. You know what I say?"

Ruth nodded and adjusted the dark, mirrored glasses, realizing that she needn't worry about looking at anything because she could look wherever she wanted—at Orion, say, on the couch.

The room was moist. She felt drops slipping down her arm, small beads of redolent sweat. She wanted to wipe them away, identify the flavor with a furtive whiff, but Orion sat on the couch, and Eva had her hands, murmuring in that strangely affected voice which promised good fortune and surprise.

"You've had some bad, bad luck. Very bad, but most of your bad I think is over. That's good. Your luck, bad, has hurt you. You should trust people more. You know what I say?"

Ruth knew what she said but wondered what it meant. Her jaw cramped, and she wished the fan above her would spin faster, would spin the air in the room and dry her arms. She told herself to pay attention.

"Many people love you, but you . . . but you I think love only one . . ." Orion sat smiling, on the couch, his ears cocked like a dog. "But I think you have not met this person yet. No," she said. "Not yet. You know what I say? I say you must trust more, be successful; open your own venture, maybe. Enjoy the luck while it last. Now," said Eva, leaving Ruth's hands and leaning forward, "you ask me questions!"

And her head was full of them—those things she wanted to ask but was afraid to know, and she wanted not to be here all over again. She wanted Eva to be wrong. She wanted Orion to quit smiling and she turned to face him, this man who was planning on traveling through Peru.

"Will you please leave?" she said.

———————

She had returned the courtesy, had left the room so Orion could ask about private matters. She sat in a room and listened to a television, gazing at a high ceiling with its own fan. She tried to count the revolutions.

On their way home, they stopped at a co-op and picked up sprouts and mushrooms; Orion was hungry, and he wouldn't eat meat. Outside the street was hot from the sun. She could feel the heat rising up through the soles of her shoes. When everything was this hot, she thought, the heat came from the earth, not the sky. It's the earth that gives and takes.

"Orion," she asked, "what are you going to do in Peru?"

"I don't know, really. Walk a lot, build canoes. There're a lot of rivers in Peru."

"But what are you going to do?"

"Shoot pictures, mostly. That's what I'm good at."

She lit a cigarette and leaned into his shoulder. "Do you love me?" she asked.

He stopped and turned to face her, and she could see the sun behind the fringes of his black, tangled hair.

"I will if you want me to."

She smiled longer than she needed to, deciding. "My uncle," she said, "he used to take us bowling—me and my mother. He had this big leather belt with a brass buckle that said *On the Rocks*. Every weekend he'd take us till she got sick. I used to think she loved him, but he was my father's brother, and my father was dead. She hated my father because he was too good for her. She wanted to be an actress." She smiled again and looked up at him. "I just don't think it works anymore. That's all."

And then she kissed him. She nipped his lip with her teeth and laughed.

What Ruth had wanted to know was why she never kept a lover, why her septum was slowly vanishing like mist, why her life promised to be so short—as if it were feeding off her strength. Instead she had asked, "What am I afraid of?"

And Eva had whispered back, "Yourself. You are afraid to love yourself. No?"

"This stuff is great," Orion said, sniffling once, twice, wiping his nose with his thumb while passing the supplies down from the bed. "But one of these days you're going to get yourself into some serious shit."

She sat in her dry, wooden chair. She gathered her kimono and smiled because she felt fresh and damp from her shower, because sometimes Orion was so naive. "I read," she said. "I keep you happy."

She set an anthology of Romantic poetry on the floor, took the straw and aligned it on a mirror with a stenciled Minnie Mouse. The second line intersected Minnie's throat and stopped just short of her crotch.

And soon the cocaine began to take effect, and she felt herself swelling with a sudden and unexpected resolve. With this she could see into the life of things, her mind made quiet while the world roared. She could read Wordsworth the way Eva had read her hand. Truth happened because experience made it; because each shaped the other; because a woman died after she lived, turned into shit, and nourished plants—

"Hey. Hey!" Orion said, looking down from the bed, the camera over his face. "Want to know what I asked?"

She leaned back and crossed her legs. She touched her thigh. After the shutter snapped, she listened to the camera setting her up for another frame, and she decided once again that she loved this feeling, this rushing fast while she sat so purposeful and calm. So polite and still.

"What did you ask?"

"Nothing. I asked her nothing! Figured she wouldn't know if I did, and I didn't want to make her lie."

She could feel him staring now, could feel him pulling away and feel the cocaine burrowing into her mind—hot like a flame and equally bright, a searing and indefatigable flash. Eternity made real, here, inside her quiet mind screaming loud, inside her room with the bed swaying overhead while Orion rifled through the sheets looking for his lens cap or socks. With the vegetation outside and the heat like sweat—a layer of thin, vanishing film.

Orion's feet hit the wooden floor, and she listened to him

leave for the shower, adjust the pipes, listened to the fall of the water—isolating the pattern of each stream until he stood before her: naked, wet, his hands cupping his ears.

"She said I shouldn't," he said.

Eyes open, wider now, trying not to blink: "Shouldn't what?"

"She said I shouldn't go!"

She sighed. She stroked his stomach with the back of her thumb, upwardly, watching her thumb and the path it made across his skin.

"Orion," she said, "I really think it's time."

Her uncle had delivered ice in Sausalito. Each Sunday after Mass he'd come over to her mother's apartment in Oakland and say, "It's time!" Her mother had no husband and a job at Burger Town, a worried brother-in-law and maladjusted child. Her mother later turned inside herself, went insane and smashed her head on the hood of a car, bled all over the asphalt, and now, thought Ruth, doesn't have to think.

She shook the ice in her drink, licked the sweat from her glass. With her uncle time had been agonizingly still, sitting naked in his garage on a block of ice, his fat belt binding her hands. The sheer pain of ice could keep her quiet if she focused on it. Sometimes he'd crush his cigar and she'd feel the spray and sizzle of coal on ice; sometimes the ice would melt, a small puddle around herself. Still the uncle would smile, would watch her skin grow blue, would promise to stop if she wouldn't tell. She told and her uncle, a flaccid man with inarticulate shoulders, continued to deliver ice. Meanwhile, she kept herself void and uncertain while her mother slept in a locked ward; while she put herself through school and counseled victims of incest; while she dealt cocaine, waiting for something she wasn't sure of.

Eva had told her to watch for a man with prematurely balding hair, had said he would bring her *much happy and fear*. But her uncle wore a hairpiece now and dated a paralegal. Eva said every day she would know more, but Ruth knew already what she wanted—she knew pain was truth, truth was unavoidable, pain was unavoidable like truth in a vacuum where time stood still. Mr. Fennerstrom had said truth was the place where we would all end up, and this, she thought, was the future for which she would wait while Orion stirred, rolling over beside her, drugged and asleep. He had finished off half the vodka.

The ice made her teeth ache fine. She set the glass on her chest, resting the lip on her chin. She drew a finger through the condensation, beaded and clear, and wiped it on the sheets. She felt comfortable here, in the wet spot, the cool moist deposit of their sex: Orion's haunches bucking with her own, in time and out, a rock and roll fortified by coke, senseless and numb as her own hot flesh which just couldn't feel anymore the galvanized chain she'd grip with the curve of her wrists.

Ruth listened to the roll and swell of Orion's breath. She liked this house, this room with its unfinished drywall and vast view of all that remained outside. From here, the ocean wasn't far away, and now in the light of a thick vanilla candle she could see her reflection, and what she really looked like if she wanted to look.

In the morning Orion would leave with a hangover and his film for Peru. They both agreed now it was time. When her jaw began to feel tight, she swallowed the remains of her drink and drew herself a pair of lines: did them up right. She wouldn't sleep but she didn't need to. She moved the candle closer and lit a cigarette. The smoke seared her sinuses, announcing she was still in fact alive; accelerated and numb, it mattered not. The proof of one's life lay in her death and the trees which might spread out and over a soul. In Peru the trees were like jungles, the bodies would rot in a river, turn into silt like the Nile or the Mississippi. In Arizona, where she had once lived, the Salt was dry and full of rocks. Dammed up and dead.

Outside, it was almost dawn and still very dark. Quiet before the sunrise, the candlelight glanced off the window. She took the candle and held it over Orion's back, pouring the molten wax and drawing the shape of a heart. He didn't stir and she allowed it to dry, cooling the wax with her breath. The wax, she realized, looked like semen.

And if you looked into the future, you had to watch it by yourself. She released a drag from her cigarette, stoked the coal and placed the bright ash inside the center of her heart.

"This one's for her," she said, waiting, while her hair grazed her breast. "This one's for you . . . And this one's for me," she said, before she crushed the butt in his spine. Before she kissed the three stars on his back with her mouth.

A I R

Cass, 1986

I keep waiting for something, like mail. From my window I watch the city set about building its new freeway, an exit ramp spilling off to L.A. I watch fire fighters across town shoot high arcs of water on a gutted Mexican restaurant. The guy next to me doesn't watch the window, just the roof, the white sheets. My girlfriend eats buffalo wings and says he won't close his eyes. They keep him juiced with morphine and turn him every six hours to shift the pain. I hear only his nurses, sometimes a priest, never him except when it hurts bad. When his ex-wife calls, I say he doesn't feel like talking. I say I'm his doctor, try writing. Still, she wants my prognosis: the truth, no matter how hard. I tell her the check's in the mail.

Sometimes I think, This is downtown Phoenix.

My brother wires from Matagalpa, says he got the news, not to worry. He says he's taking lots of important pictures and that he'll be back soon. I don't get out of bed to piss anymore, I puke fruit punch and try not to think. My girlfriend transfers to Colorado State, so she can ski, and the guy next to me dies. I want to tell him the only thing we have for sure is our health, but a nurse breaks my I.V. He breaks it in the top of my wrist digging for a vein and the Mexican restaurant decides to go Italian and install fountains, two with water, when the ex-wife sends a card with green and pink birds. The nurses, they give me the card while behind blue paper masks they worry and wait. They say I need a little more weight while really just a swallow of water would be fine. Like platinum and birds. Like all those things that keep going up because once the ground starts to shake, I swear to God, you can feel it coming.

PARIS,

THE EASY WAY

Sam, 1988

I first learned the importance of air at the Casper Community Pool during my brother's thirteenth birthday party—a big one because now he had finished the eighth grade and was learning to kiss his girlfriend, also our neighbor, Sally Sconzalla. Like my brother, I had a crush on Sally, but what she could do for my brother I was still too underdeveloped to appreciate. I merely liked the way she combed her hair, which was yellow and loose, and I liked the sound of her voice.

At the Casper Community Pool she and my brother were diving from the springboard when I decided to join them. Never before had I been in water so deep. I swam my short, choppy strokes, stopping every five feet to hang onto the wall. I must have been thinking about something. Maybe I thought I was near the wall, maybe I thought the water was shallow. Either way, I took in half the pool, the air washed out of my lungs, and my body caught on—this was not the proper way to float. I couldn't hear anything but the water, and my voice in the water, but I'm sure it was Sally who saw me. I was lifted out of the pool with one arm by a big, tan lifeguard. Later, when Sally wrapped me in her towel and told me I would be all right, this is what I learned. I learned that when our lungs are filled with something they shouldn't be, no one, not even the person we decide to love most in the world, will ever hear us. This was back in Wyoming, during the summer of 1965, where we were all still growing up under a sky the size of history and equally dull.

As a kid watching *Star Trek*, I used to wait for something new to happen: an unfamiliar spaceship, a forceful encounter, things suddenly appearing as soon as the ship's viewscreen was turned on. Now I'm wondering who cleaned the viewscreen, the big windshield they drove behind. I think even space must have debris the way the West has dust.

The windshield wipers on my truck have smeared the dust into mud, and thirty, maybe forty miles ahead, somewhere beyond Trinidad, lightning rips open the sky—long brilliant seams opening for just a moment the possibilities beyond our own atmosphere.

Lightning, gravity, love—I've never properly understood any of it.

I went to college. During the '81 recession, when I couldn't get a job, I did the circuit well enough to break even. For two years

I was an overpaid stable manager in Sedona. In my old office, which was really a tack room full of broken-down saddles and loose stirrups, hangs a recent photograph of Sally. She is sitting on a beach in Monaco, her top off, her face angled towards the sea, and on the back she has written "You'd really love it here."

I decided to leave the Boynton Canyon Resort the day after I received Sally's picture, the day old man McClenahan showed up early for his ride. His face had been detailed by the sun, by age and the weather, and I watched the lines shift in his face while he grew angry with me because I hadn't yet grained his mare, Cleo.

"It's climbing," he said, pointing at the sun. "It's climbing. Where's my Cleo!"

I fed his horse, offered him coffee while we waited. Mrs. McClenahan wouldn't be by to pick him up until noon for lunch and his nap. After his ride, after he'd finished brushing Cleo down, he would ask me to inspect a hoof, trim a frog. Later he'd wander around behind me and talk with the guests or help Gomez with his English. And it was hard to dislike either, the old horse or the old man.

But that morning as we sat in the tack room, drinking coffee and enjoying the morning, the lingering smells of hay and shit and grain dust, the old man grew serious.

"Hey, good buddy," he said.

"Hey," I said.

"When you gonna leave?"

"Leave where, Mac?"

"Leave," he said, nodding toward the door. "When you gonna leave? You know."

"No," I said. "I don't know."

"Cleo, her lungs are about to bust."

"They're fine," I said. "Just a little used up."

"Used up? They're all used up with the heaves. No. Maybe," he said, shaking his head. He began to laugh and looked at the picture of Sally over my desk. "Not like her," he said, laughing. "Not like her, good buddy."

The old man left for his ride, Gomez showed up hungover and late, and I took out a pair of tourists: a husband and wife team from Phoenix, newly married by the looks. They made jokes and giggled while I told them about all the cowboys Rooster had crippled back in his prime. The man kept a sharp lookout for rattlesnakes and occasional mountain lions, and I thought about the old man and his mare, Cleo, combing the countryside next to Highway 89A looking for something vaguely familiar and safe. The old man had kids, he said, only he didn't know where they were, which is why I suppose he told me.

After the incident at the Casper Community Pool, it was decided I would learn to swim as well as I did my chores or homework. My father would drive me into Casper to an indoor pool for weekly lessons, where I would wear black nylon suits and take instruction from people not much older than my brother or Sally. Once, after a lesson, while waiting in a public hallway for my dad, I watched him pull up to the curb. I had been waiting with the others and I left them to meet my dad halfway across the snow and ice. The cold made my hair freeze. My dad waved, slipped and fell. He fell about as gracefully as a horse—scrambling, all legs and panic, trying to pretend that either this hadn't happened or that he did this all the time. I could hear the kids laughing through the still open door. He waved again, this time to the kids behind me, patting at his hip as if feeling for injury.

In the truck he breathed heavily and gripped the steering wheel. "Whew," he said, trying to laugh. "Your old man's not as limber as he used to be."

And I think what I felt then was my embarrassment shift to worry, to a slight tremor of mortality. Hearing my dad call himself old meant he would only get older and, eventually, leave me to myself. In the water, after nearly drowning, I had been frightened, but I was not frightened by death. The fear was too inarticulate to be specific.

"Dad," I said, "you're not an old man!"

And really he wasn't. He was the same age I am now, but when we feel as if we're getting old, there's not much that's going to change that feeling. My father is now fifty-two. He raises some of the finest Morgans in Wyoming and he raises his grandson, Robert, much in the same way he raised me. Only now he really isn't as limber as he used to be. I suppose in truth no one really is.

Why didn't I marry Sally Sconzalla? I guess because my brother already had. My brother was like one of those ensigns or corpsmen who open up every episode of *Star Trek*. The nameless one we've never seen before. The one who beams down with the landing party and gets lost or vaporized by misunderstanding aliens. My brother enlisted in 1970, was beamed down into Cambodia, and disappeared without a trace.

As for the old man, he combed the hillside with his mare while I told the tourists stories. When I returned the tourists to the barn, Gomez took their money and told them to have a nice day. I stood at the corral and watched them leave, walking nervously between the loose horses while I stood behind and admired the man's wife. I watched one horse prepare to kick another. I watched the old man rub down Cleo and lead her into a paddock. Later that afternoon, a large group of realtors from Tucson was scheduled for a ride and cookout: Gomez would meet us at the site with hamburgers and beer, and later he'd take out his guitar to sing love songs from Ethiopia. In the office he sat in my chair, his feet propped on my desk, leafing through a book entitled *Paris, the Easy Way*.

"*Bonjour,*" he said. "*Comment ça va!*"

"Fine," I said. I poured coffee and asked about the status of a horse with fistulous withers, so bad the pus still ran after six weeks—a lingering, festering sore caused by an ill-fitting saddle.

"She sure is pretty," Gomez said, rising from the chair and pointing at the picture of Sally. "Pretty like my sister, you know. *Bonita. Tres belle.* Ohh la la."

I drank my coffee, brown and badly burnt, and studied the picture while Gomez loaded up an injection of Combiotic. He pulled down from a shelf the hydrogen peroxide.

"I gonna play darts now," he said, referring to the syringe. "And you gonna feel sad for a while. But you get over it. *Ciao.*"

A month before, Gomez had been Italian; he'd take a green card anywhere. He left while I sat and considered the photograph of Sally. I considered the slow curve of her flank. In the photograph she has a neck like an antelope, and I thought about my father's hayloft where she told me what to do without ever telling me, as if between us someone had strung a fine wire, a telegraph of instruction, of unexpected urgency and regret. Later she left Wyoming to teach at a Catholic school in Dallas, and my brother never came home, which is something I think we each always knew even when we didn't know it. Maybe he was gone too long for any of us to remember clearly. Who knows what we really used to know?

One thing I know is this: if confined, a horse under a sky with lightning is a dangerous thing. It wants only to run because the lightning is too inexplicable, too close to the bone to be considered safe from even a distance. A horse reacts to lightning the way a stud will a mare, and the coupling of horses is not a simple enterprise.

Right now the weather grows temporarily safe. The sky blisters with ions, waiting for rain, and the air is so clear it looks like glass—it's that transparent. The Colorado border smells like rain, like creosote and dust, and I know Sebastian, my own horse in the trailer behind me, is no longer frightened because I, too, am no longer frightened.

———————

We can only know what we once didn't know. At my brother's wedding, I was the best man because his best friend had already been shipped to Asia, and our father thought it would be nice this way. Sally was dressed like an angel, I stood behind my brother, and at the proper time I held out the ring he'd spent six months saving for. It was a pretty gold ring. A wedding ring, he'd explained, and chock-full of meaning.

We stood up against a fence and watched my father work a yearling; my brother, just in from town, took the ring out of the box to show me. The dust from the corral floated all around us, but it never touched the ring. The ring was still too new for dust. "Do you see how it's round?" he said. "That's the meaningful part. The finger is the man and the ring is the woman, and once you're married the two go at it forever, and as long as you wear your ring you can never go at it with anyone else or the whole deal gets all shot to hell."

———————

I found the old man face down in the paddock with a fly on his neck. The horses had circled away from him and he lay in the orange dirt alone. I rolled him over and searched for a pulse. I beat on his chest. I cleared his airway and removed a loose denture. I began to breathe. I beat again on his chest, losing count, searching for his heart because I wasn't sure where it was. I felt his ribs crack beneath my hands and knew I was going to have to breathe into him again—my mouth on his, his lips rough and smelling of garlic and decay and later the whiff of his gut rising up through the throat while I kept breathing into his lungs. I felt them rise while mine collapsed. After a while, I realized he was supposed to be dead, and so I left him in the paddock under the sun with the horses still frightened by the suddenness and smell of death.

———————

By nature, a horse has only three gaits; the others are learned. After work each day Gomez and I would go to the Oak Creek Tavern, order a pitcher and shoot pool. Last summer, though, the local network in Chicago began showing reruns of *Star Trek*— the same reruns I had watched in college, the same episodes I had watched as a kid in Wyoming. So instead of playing 8-ball, I began to reacquaint myself with plots and character traits: who was logical, who was emotional, who was both, which was really all of us. The tavern had a satellite hookup, and watching all these episodes reminded me of the '60s and how hopeful and naive we were all becoming while I was still completely unaware of the world which had created it—Ford Mustang, Simon and Garfunkel, the race for the moon.

I once lived with a woman in Santa Fe. I ran a barn for Lazarus Arabians, where I was instructed by the part-time owners of syndicated studs on the proper music for mares about to foal (Mozart, piped through the stalls with air-conditioning), where I learned to keep my mouth shut and watch people make wise investments. At home it was worse. The woman would paint bad imitations of Georgia O'Keeffe and read D. H. Lawrence, nonstop, reading aloud always the passages which had to do with men and horses and lust until, finally, she asked me to marry her. It was the first time I'd ever been asked, and the next day I gave my notice.

———————

I gave Gomez the blender, my contribution to the barn since I was going to argue with the owner of the Boynton Canyon Resort that, illegal or not, Gomez most deserved the blender. Make him the boss, I would say; the tourists will like the color. They would like the color the way they liked the rocks of Sedona—the red, angry cliffs shaped by the wind into the names of things like Coffee Pot, like Cathedral and Bell.

We sat in the tack room and drank margaritas. Paul Harvey was over, and I advised Gomez to get rid of the horse with bad withers, and to get rid of Cleo, too; sell her quick and send the money to Mrs. McClenahan. "Do it right," I said, "and she'll send you a bottle."

"*Oui*," said Gomez, looking almost lost. "But what about her?" He pointed at the picture of Sally on the wall. Right up there by Will Rogers and a bilingual notice to employees, she really was a fine addition to the wall. It seemed to me she'd do more good on the wall in Boynton Canyon than she would anywhere else.

"I had to kill a horse once," I said. "It ran through a fence and nearly cut off its leg. It wasn't worth the vet bills. The leg would never heal, so I shot it in the head just like the movies. I shot it in the head with a Remington I had to borrow, but the bad part wasn't killing it. The bad part was figuring out what to do next. How do you move a dead horse?"

"Slowly," said Gomez, nodding.

"I put a chain around its neck and drug it out of the corral with a Jeep. I called the foundry, the guy couldn't pick it up for two days. I covered the horse with a ground cloth and put wagon wheels against it—decorations, you know, to please the guests. Four days later it was still there, rising like a balloon—this dead horse covered with wagon wheels and plastic and flies. But what I remember most was wrapping the chain around its neck and pulling it out of the mud with the Jeep. The chain left marks in the neck. When the guy finally showed up he had to pull her on a flatbed with a winch."

After my brother finished basic training, he came home on leave. His hair was short, he wore green clothes, and he spent most of his time with Sally in the big room our father had fixed up just for them. A week later we drove him to the airport where he would catch a plane to Alaska and then pick up a transport going somewhere else. We stood at the gate, my father and Sally and me, and said good-bye. My brother had something special to say to everyone, and he told me to take care of the family, to watch over Dad and the ranch. "We got problems U.T.A.," he said. "But we got you. Take care of Sally," he said. And then he whispered something into Sally's ear, kissed her on the mouth, and walked away up the runway. On the way home, my father pulled over the truck to let me drive, and Sally turned on the radio.

I attended McClenahan's funeral, of course. It was Catholic, long and overcrowded. I saw lawyers and doctors and people who had flown to Sedona from New York and Boston and Chicago in private airplanes. A memorial service was held outdoors beneath the shadow of Bell Rock, a large and brightly colored geological oddity—a source of crystals, of immeasurable energy, swollen with meaning and mystery for the new age.

Mrs. McClenahan was a handsome woman. She stood among these people I would never know and listened to them say nice things about her husband.

"Mac was very fond of you," she said to me.

"I'm sorry," I said.

"He said you always took good care of Cleo. You reminded him of our boys."

But the boys were not present. I had learned one of them was dead, the other in a foreign country. I told Mrs. McClenahan not to worry about Cleo, and she looked at me sadly, as if there were no reason why she ever should. Later that afternoon the body was shipped on a private plane to a cemetery in Illinois.

———————

I think being in space must be like being in water: there is no air. The rain is hard now. It washes over the shell of the truck like a river; it films the windows and the wipers beat at the rain like oars. Denver is still a long way north. I feel the tires skim over flat spots on the road where water stands, and I adjust my speed accordingly.

———————

After I found the old man, after I'd cracked his ribs and breathed into his lungs, I went to the barn and had a drink. I called the ambulance, said they didn't need to rush. I called Mrs. McClenahan.

She arrived before the paramedics. She drove her big car straight past the barn and up to the paddock. Her hair, streaked with gray, glimmered in the light; her face was pale as a woman's breast.

And I watched her go to her husband. She knelt on her heels, cocked in the dirt, and reached for his hand, which must have felt unexpectedly cool. The sun was hot, the hand cool, and by the time the paramedics had arrived, she knew where she wanted him sent. I brought her into the barn, the tack room, where she sat very still in my chair while I poured her a shot of whiskey. She held the cup in her hands and stared at the coffee stains on the cheap porcelain as if trying to identify the shapes.

"Once," she said. "Once before, I thought he was dead. I had to make sure."

"He had a nice ride," I said.

"Yes," she said, nodding, "I'm sure he did."

I watched her watch her drink. The rings on her hands pinched her fingers, grown swollen with age, and I watched the rings pinch her fingers, thinking someday the rings are going to slip loose because that's what life does. It eats away at us until we're empty.

––––––––––

Space may very well be the final frontier, but in what direction should we travel? Right now I'm going home, traveling north, which on a map is not as far away as it seems—a few days' drive up I-25. It's as easy as sending a half-naked picture of yourself through the mail. And while I think about everyone I've ever known and probably damaged, one way or another, this is what I think about most: I think about the old man I couldn't save, the old man lying quietly inside his sealed box, unable to go anywhere but in, inside himself to the core of what he once was. He lies in a grave somewhere in Illinois and he keeps going inside himself, because now when it matters most he can't get out. He can't get out, so he goes in. He goes in, deep inside himself, so deep until he finally discovers that maybe the space around the living is more important than any of us ever thought. Because maybe after a while there really is no place left for us to go.

IN THE LAND OF
MILK AND HONEY
AND JELL-O

1301 Ash

For Betsy, gifts are spontaneous, full of promise and possibility. On St. Patrick's Day she bought a green cotton camisole. After her lessons, she showered and dressed in a linen skirt, the camisole. She set loose her hair and walked uptown to the bar where Miles worked. The sun felt warm on her legs. Inside were inflated pink flamingos and people she knew. The light was dusty and yellow from the late afternoon sun, and she walked up to the bar to order a green beer.

"Hi, Mister," she said. "I brought you a surprise!"

Later that night, while celebrating St. Patrick's Day and the life they were making for each other, Miles decided to buy Betsy a bicycle.

———————

The house at 1301 Ash was built by a man who designed an inexpensive way to manufacture fiberglass bathtubs. He had it built for his fiancée, had the workers install Mexican tile, large bay windows, and three oversized fiberglass tubs. The backyard is private and surrounded by citrus trees.

Adjacent to the kitchen is a guest house, a studio apartment which Miles and Betsy rent out to a fine arts student from Maui. The main house they keep sparsely furnished; they keep their desks in the dining room; in the living room they keep the television, video machine, recording equipment and piano. The television is very small, a 9-inch screen which lends itself best to serious dramas without subtitles.

The art student's name is Max. She wears black clothes, long silver earrings, and cropped Polynesian hair—a mane which has been recently shaved, leaving a single, attenuated braid. At night she comes into the house to watch rented movies with Miles and Betsy. Every half hour or so, they pause the machine while she steps outside for a cigarette because Miles has recently quit. When it is too cool to step outside, she goes to her studio and looks at her paintings while she smokes. To get by, she does her friends' hair. She keeps special scissors in a leather case. Usually, she cuts hair on the driveway, and when she is finished she sweeps the driveway with a broom so no one will track any hair into the house. She also gets money from a trust fund.

———————

Betsy has lovely hair. It is thick and full of color. It is the color, Miles thinks, of mystery and tradition—red, yellow and orange all at once. At night she uses it to wake him, her hair flowing along the edges of his body. Over the years it has become as much a part of their language as silence.

————

Miles lets Max in on the secret. He takes her with him to help pick out the bicycle, and the one they pick comes from Japan. The components, the frame, the cables and grease and paint job all come from Japan, shipped overseas in pieces to be packaged in Oklahoma and later assembled in Tempe, Arizona.

Miles agrees to buy the bicycle on layaway. Each month he walks up University to make his payment—sixty-seven dollars and forty-six cents, and after each payment a sales person gives him a plastic water bottle. The employees at the bicycle shop vary in stature and age, but they all wear nylon bicycle shorts, and they all have monstrously thick thighs. The men who race shave their legs to fight wind resistance. They ride bicycles with Italian names and look like they know what they're doing.

————

Behind the citrus trees, twenty feet beyond the property line, run the railroad tracks. Regular as clockwork, the freights run along and keep them all in rhythm. When a train comes by, it makes the house shake, and everyone stops talking until it passes. On Sundays, Betsy makes bag lunches and walks up the tracks to 10th Street. She leaves the lunches beneath the metal arch of the rail crossing gate. Inside the lunches she leaves condoms and information about local shelters, and each week the lunches disappear.

————

One night Max announces that she has been assigned a final project in Modern Foundries: she is going to do a series of women's breasts in Jell-O, she is going to call the project *In the Land of Milk and Honey and Jell-O*.

"So," she says, "it will be very archetypal."

The next morning in the backyard, Max mixes up a batch of plaster of paris. Betsy spreads a blanket on the grass, removes her shirt and lies on her back while Max begins to apply the plaster.

"Yes," says Max, nodding. "Yes."

At first the plaster feels warm, but as the mixture hardens it begins to cool. Miles sits on the blanket to watch. He sips from his coffee and asks about flavors.

"Lime? Orange? I really like raspberry," he says.

"Raspberry for you," Max says.

"Raspberry," says Betsy, giggling.

"Don't," Max says. "You'll shift the cast."

"Promise," says Betsy.

"Here," says Max. She puts Miles' hand on the cooling cast. "Hold this."

Betsy wipes a strand of hair from her face, leaving a white streak along her cheek, and Miles holds onto the mold. He feels the plaster growing stiff beneath the shape of his fingers.

"It's weird," Betsy whispers. "I can't feel you this way, but I really want to. I really want to, Mister."

Citizen & the Second Hands

By Easter the evenings stay warm. They move the VCR and television outside to the porch to watch movies; now Max can smoke and they can watch movies without ever having to hit the *Pause*.

And things are looking up for Miles. He is invited to join a pseudo-punk band: they need a guitar player who can double on bass and the synthesizer. The members of the band all wear makeup and clothes bought from thrift shops. Because Miles is tired of tending bar and reading novels, he decides to give the band a try, but he still keeps his job at the bar. The name of the band is Citizen & the Second Hands. They rehearse weeknights in the drummer's garage, and on his way home, first through the dim, quiet streets of Old Tempe, and then along the tracks to 1301 Ash, he wonders about the names of things.

––––––––––

Today, while well into her sixth lesson, Betsy marvels at her patience, her own patience which she must have inherited from someone she doesn't know. Joey Humbert, her student, struggles through eight difficult measures of Brahms, and she has him repeat these measures because while he's repeating she can think. Today she is restless and cool, eager to have this over with. Outside, through the open doors, the orange blossoms bloom and fill the air. The room is empty save for the piano and appliances, the wires from the appliances which wander through the room like scattered shoelaces. The carpet is a soft cream. The sun throws shadows through the blinds across the soft carpet, and Joey Humbert stops playing.

"Tell me a story," he says.

"Play," she says, tapping at the sheet music. "Play."

––––––––––

At the bar he hears a story. It is a story about a man who lost his teeth in a bicycle accident: a bus passed him on the road, he got sucked up in the afterwash, he hit a metal sign. "Buses are death, Man," says the man telling the story.

While rinsing glasses, Miles catches himself looking at the man's teeth. He considers telling a joke. He wants to know by what authority he has to worry about buses. He imagines Betsy on the side of the road, the pink and blue Japanese bicycle scratched, bent, shorn by a passing fender. Meanwhile, the smell of bleach rises up from the water, and he thinks it a clean, refreshing smell.

———————

That night in bed Miles asks Betsy what she wants most in the world right now.

"Me," she says, pausing to look up. "I want me."

It seems to him a peculiar thing to say, considering she's doing such a fine job. This is not a thing he expected her to say.

———————

During breakfast Max brings into the house one of her recent self-portraits: a slender figure holding a lance astride a silver horse against swirling, tropical colors.

"It's from a different age," she says. "*Max Throughout the Centuries.* I thought you'd like it."

"I like it," Miles says, looking thoughtfully. "Is it archetypal?"

"God," Max says, looking at Betsy. "You have great hair."

———————

It is dark and Miles is walking home along the railroad tracks, one tie at a time, when he pauses to look at a house surrounded by lean trees and a broken-down fence. Beyond the fence is a yard and large wooden porch. The porch surrounds the house, which has wide, open windows. Behind one of the windows lies a girl with black hair. She lies on top of a bed, reading a book, and sometimes before turning a page she stops to brush her hair from her eyes. Sometimes she lights a cigarette or pauses to take a drag from one she has already lit. Overhead he hears airplanes preparing for their descent into Phoenix, and he knows a train is coming soon.

For Betsy's birthday, they threw a party. The backyard filled with friends and neighbors, including the girl who read books, though no one knew who she was exactly. Some thought they recognized her from the bar, which seemed to make sense. Meanwhile everyone drank beer and ate Jell-O from the molds Max had made. Everyone agreed the Jell-O was a big hit. When everybody left, Miles gave Betsy her new blue and pink Japanese bicycle, and Betsy had no idea what to say.

The following two days he avoided her. He worked extra hours at the bar, he practiced alone in his room, he even took up walking along the tracks to stop and watch the girl who read books. He thought about taking the bicycle back and getting a refund, but he wanted Betsy to grow to like it. And later, after he forgot about it, after he no longer had a reason to practice more than he should, Miles began to take more and more walks.

The Vision

In May the air begins to smell like semen, and things are tense. Miles is sullen and depressed; Betsy, fitful and confused; Max, puzzled but nonetheless prolific. She works at her art daily and fills the house with her canvases: Max as Shepherdess, Max as Sailor, Max as Welder. Each century grows more and more difficult to discern, and the canvases are vast, full of movement and space and herself. When Betsy will let her, Max braids her hair into long, thin braids and talks about how much she loves her hair, about how what she needs most is vision to see things the way others don't.

A desert in the ocean, she says. An ocean in the desert.

Today while doing laundry, Miles first emptied the dryer full of clothes belonging to Max. He took her T-shirts and jeans and socks and underwear, folding them into loose shapes, piling them in the wicker basket, when he came across a green cotton camisole. At first he didn't know what to do, but later that night he decided it would be best if he moved into his own bedroom for a while to think things out.

———————

When Max cut his hair, she did it in the backyard on the grass so she wouldn't have to sweep it up. He sat in a lawn chair with a towel around his neck while Max buzzed the shaver over his neck and around his ears. By the time she was finished, his hair was short like a cadet's with three strips of scalp.

"For decoration," Max said. "You'll surprise Bets. She won't know who you are."

"Yeah," he said, "but how does it look?"

———————

Citizen & the Second Hands gets a gig at The Banana Republic on 16th Street where the cover is steep. It is their first gig and the band is skittish and uncertain. For a while, playing in the dimly lit club, they try to cover their mistakes—a faulty bridge, a misplaced riff—until it becomes clear that the people inside care more about the atmosphere, which is warm and close and dim. Here the people dance as fast as the music itself. They dance a pseudo-punk slam in expensive sneakers, tops, and knee-length shorts.

While he takes over the board, Miles watches Betsy and Max dance, the space between them when they move, and for a while he thinks about the girl in the house who reads books in the light of a room. During the break he sits with people he knows and drinks a beer. They say the band is great, everybody loves it.

"Yeah," Max says, "you guy's are really hot."

Sometimes he catches others looking at him strangely, and he remembers that Max has recently cut his hair.

Betsy agrees to sit in on keyboards until they find someone else, but she doesn't really want to. She wants to go back to school and do a Ph.D. In the mail she receives catalogue after catalogue with information on fellowships and awards. Now, in the evenings, instead of watching movies together, Max works in her room and Betsy reviews for the Graduate Record Exam. When he's not rehearsing, Miles continues to take his walks. Eventually Betsy receives an application from the University of Texas, Austin, and a letter from her brother whose wife left him years ago. In the letter he explains that he has joined A.A., and that their stepfather, Norm, is recently dead from a stroke while driving a cab in Buffalo. She never even knew he had a cab, she had thought he was in L.A., and the news of his death drives her into a depression which will last for months, a depression so profound she will be entirely unaware of its depth. She will know only that everything still changes all around her.

Tonight the girl doesn't read, and she's not alone. She sits outside on the big wooden porch with a boy and talks to the boy about why he never writes and what she's going to do. After they stop talking for a while the girl pulls a futon onto the porch beneath the stars and moon with all the trees nearby. The trees nearby and then the train, a long one, rumbling behind and overhead a jet, and then another, falling into the city's flight path. Here, with all the trees and stars and moon, and the girl with skin like milk, the boy doesn't seem to mind the traffic. Not here, not under the heat—the girl, the boy, the moon under the stars watching, watching, watching for the train, the boy's pants and all these trees and all these faces and the boy's pants, which Miles takes to let them know we're not alone.

"What's that?" says the boy.

"Shhh," says the girl, beginning to lift. "It's just the train."

———

Max brings home her friend Rosa, and together they sit outside watching a foreign film on the VCR. They sit together on the couch and invite Betsy to join them, which she does after first making cocoa, then lacing the cocoa with Kahlua. They sit on the couch and watch the movie drinking cocoa, and after a while Miles comes home and goes into the bathroom.

When the movie is over, Betsy knocks at the door, but Miles doesn't answer. She knocks again, but still no answer. Finally Max gets a butter knife, but only Rosa can make it work, can make the knife slip through the lock, the lock shift, the door slide open where Miles sits in the big fiberglass tub. On the edge of the tub lie three disposable razors. The tub is filled with water and blood, his scalp covered with soap. His head is entirely shaved, and a long, bloody gash is welling up over his ear.

"What do you want?" he says. "Just what the hell do you want?"

The Sky

Before Miles loaded up his pack to take a trip across America, Max drove Betsy to the airport. Then Max moved with Rosa into the main house, and Miles took the studio. Because Max had found someone to love, she also found a new subject, and she began a project entitled *Rosa Throughout the Centuries*. For a while, Miles kept his job at the bar. Sometimes the girl with skin like milk came by, sometimes with people he knew, though Miles never saw the boy with no pants, and he took to watching Max and Rosa because it was easier somehow if you knew who you were watching, easier and full of more risk and maybe even intimacy. It taught him things about himself he never thought he knew, and after a while, after he began to feel better about things, he hitched a ride toward Wickenberg.

But what he'd think about most, later, when he was on the road waiting for a ride south of Burlington, or Des Moines, was this:

Once, before everything began to fall apart, Betsy woke Miles in the night. She led him outside through the sliding glass doors into the yard. Once outside, they lay on their backs naked looking up at the sky for all the world to see. The air was heavy with blossoms, the night warm like a mouth, and beneath their blanket they could feel the grass beneath the weight of their bodies. The sky was close, heavy with haze and warm, and they lay on their backs very still watching the sky.

"This is what it feels like," Betsy had said.

"What?"

"The sky," she said, closing her eyes. "This is what it feels like when the sky is falling in."

S W A N S

Walt, 1989

Beneath the roof of the porch we were safe. We watched the hard rain fall, long silver threads you could easily tangle yourself up in. Threads you could see only in the light from a streetlamp or a lone, lit window across the way. Otherwise, the rain was invisible. You could only hear it or see the next day the shape of its drops etched in the paint of your car.

Brian played catch with Liz in the street. They stood apart and threw a football: Brian, twenty feet towards the dark: Liz, near my car, clapping, catching the ball once, twice. It was too slippery for her to always grab hold, too big and difficult to see. It dwarfed her hands which, in the light, looked hopeful, like wings. She wore a sodden skirt and tank top and no shoes. She threw the ball like a girl.

In the rain Brian looked soft. He was in love. Before I knew him, his wife was killed on the Sawmill Parkway, the car squeezed to a box with his wife inside caught between a guard-rail and an overloaded fruit truck. It took a half-hour to cut through the steel and make a door to pull her out. The traffic, he said, was backed up even longer. The highway was full of peaches which people collected while they waited for the road to clear.

They had married young, fresh from college, with separate careers which would only spiral up and give each enough money to do things together: weekends in Connecticut, afternoons at the Hyatt, theater and tennis and occasional time to read aloud to one another, in the mornings, mostly, lying in bed reading the latest novel which had come in the mail. Storybook lives until the traffic killed her. He took a severe cut in pay to try again, here, in this average city on the edge of the Midwest where now he played catch with a girl in the rain—a recent psychology graduate from the university. In the light her brown arms shimmered like oil.

"He's so happy," Helen said. She reached for our wine, filled the glasses with a fine, heavy burgundy. "I mean, just look at him."

"All gone?" I asked.

She tipped the bottle. "All gone," she said, sliding under my arm. I could smell the back of her neck, and she felt smooth and warm beneath my arm on this porch. Brian and I had bought the building to shelter our money. He took the bottom apartment; I, the second—we shared the porch and furnished it with this soft, weather-beaten sofa Helen and I sat on.

"Do you think she's pretty?" Helen asked.

"Who?"

"Liz," she said, laughing.

"She does," I said. "Can't you tell? She likes to watch herself in the mirror."

At night I liked to drive, out of the city to places I'd never been before. I'd stop at a motel lounge for a beer, a truckstop for coffee, look at people I didn't know and think about my return home: driving fast in the glow of the lights from the dash while I entered the Fort Pitt tunnel, driving through the quiet of the mountain until I came flying out over the city, its lights ablaze like creation itself—dazzling and bright and safely distant. A postcard with the name of an old lover on back. It made me happy until I'd have to park my car on the street. In time, I said, I would buy a house, which pleased Helen, this talk about my buying a house.

During the week, Helen and I would swim at the Y. Early evening, after work, before we would eat. Sometimes we would leave separately because we both needed for a while to be separate, but still we always swam. Laps. Long, hard laps. She had swum in college, had developed the stroke of one who swam: smoothly muscled, sleek, fast. In the water with her suit sealing her skin, polished into her flesh so that if it were evening, or if the light were suddenly to shift, you would have seen only the shell of her body—the determined result of months of her life spent in the water. She left the slightest of wakes, an eclipse in the shape of a woman with whom I could swim.

In short, we kept ourselves built the way we wanted, with finely muscled chests and long, flexible tendons. Helen sipped her wine and grew warm. Brian threw badly and hit a car, its hood bending beneath the weight of the football and Liz laughing hysterically. Across the street a light flicked on, a window opened. An old man poked his head into the rain.

"Quiet down!" he yelled. "Or I'm calling the cops!"

"Go ahead," Liz yelled back. "You go right ahead!"

The old man slammed his window, Brian and Liz came running up the steps laughing and dripping with rainwater. They disturbed Helen who, while not asleep, was content with the heat of her wine, lying in the crotch of my arm, the stem of her glass held loosely between her fingers like a plant.

"Walt," Brian said, "wake up!"

"I am awake," I said.

"So's everyone else," Liz said.

At this hour, though, no one should have been awake, including the old man across the street. This was his neighborhood undergoing recent development, with a new nightclub only a block away, where the four of us had just been, dancing with one another until we were drenched with sweat and cool steam which rose from the floor to look like mist; with two pricey restaurants nearby whose patrons took up the space for our cars; where people sat up late in the building across the street and watched the bars close or played catch because one wanted so desperately to please the other—an inconsiderate girl with brown skin.

I couldn't help think that Brian had made a terrible mistake. Liz pulled at the fabric of her top and let it slap her skin. She sat on the rail and gathered her skirt to wring the water out. She looked so matriarchal doing that—her legs spread, her hands between, wringing out the cloth of her skirt.

"You two need a towel," Helen said, rising. She left the porch and returned with two thick towels which read *Brian & Liz*. They dried one another with the towels we had given them, new towels which still smelled like cotton, while Helen resumed her place on the sofa and folded herself into my side. With practice, I suppose she had come to think she fit.

It's simple, really. The way things fit. Raised properly you learn to behave, to say *please* and *thank you*, to learn the right language and wear a necktie young so that later, when it matters, you absorb the fabric into yourself the way cotton will rainwater. You learn to take a sport—squash, lacrosse, it doesn't matter if you're good. Mine had been track, and our manner, our posture is all a result of our past and the way it made us grow: the way a tree in a forest will twist itself into a knot reaching for the sun; the way a man burdened with loss will allow himself to grow soft and damp in the rain; the way some women will let their hair fall into place, or curl into your side.

When the police came by, I walked out to the street. I stood in the rain which was slowing and talked with one of the cops, a black woman who seemed not to take this complaint too seriously. I apologized, said we were celebrating.

"What?" said the woman, smiling. She leaned with her arm on the door as if she were pleased with the coolness of the rain.

"My friend," I said, pointing, "he's engaged. We were a little loud."

"Well that's nice," she said.

"Just move it inside," her partner said.

I left the cruiser in the street while the woman said, "Congratulations!"—the car driving off, the tires hissing through the rainwater. I returned to the sofa where now we all sat safely tucked, no longer a public disturbance. Just two couples on the porch watching the night.

Liz said, "You know, this is just like the fair. The Tunnel of Love." She admired the stone on her finger, a brightly polished stone of medium weight.

After Brian began dating Liz, the four of us went to the amusement park. We walked in the sun on asphalt and watched people eat fried dough, pitch baseballs; where young boys in tight, sullied jeans gathered in groups to watch girls and smoke; where the four of us went through the Tunnel of Love, sitting in pairs in big plastic swans which floated down an artificial stream.

While waiting in line, Brian told us a story. "Once," he said, "my brother and I went down one of these. In New Jersey. We were too young for the big rides. Ben asked Dad why this was called the Tunnel of Love, and Dad said because this was where people kissed. When it got dark, he kissed me and I got off and told my dad next time he could go. Not me. I wasn't going to go anymore."

And Liz kissed him, hard, her body stretched tight against him while we stood waiting in line, while Helen took my hand and smiled and reminded me of how once, after we first met, I had wanted only briefly for her to do the same. For a moment she reminded me of a woman I once met at a bar. After the third drink, the woman slid her hand inside my sleeve and told me all about Monaco and Dublin, and then I realized that Helen was not this woman in any shape or form, and I wondered what it was about Helen that had made me remember something I'd just as soon well forget. Perhaps it was the sway of her hip, or the passing of some familiar cologne.

Liz was a big girl, busty, with thick bones, thick skin and long, straight hair which relied on the light for its color. Were Brian more lean, she'd squeeze the life right out of him, and there, beneath the yellow light of the porch, her hair looked like beer.

"Goodnight," Helen said, rising, taking my hand. She wanted me to follow. Near Brian and Liz, Helen would grow wanton and loose, watching them made her turn ripe like a pomegranate. She kissed them each, brushed my hand again, leaving, and I said, "In a while," because I needed to wait until I was ready: sleep, with the hum of the city behind my eyes and Helen nearby, breathing softly like a clock while I slept couched in the arms of a Soma, or Thorazine, a Halcion. Sleep, like research or death, is something we each do alone. In the morning, Helen and I would wake early to lift, to apply our muscle groups differently. Her eyes would be foggy with wine, but they would clear as she began to focus, and I would watch her through the moves, her body strapped inside a machine with her limbs articulate and full of a sudden, hidden strength.

That night, however, in the twilight of Liz and Brian's celebration, I don't think I really thought about sleep. Instead, I thought if I'd ever been married, never would I be able to replace my wife, the way I knew my parents sitting in their soft, private rooms in strange, foreign cities would never be able to replace their son. Perhaps they thought about me as much as they thought about each other, or the time my father brought home his boyfriend, Steve, and my mother slashed his cheek with a broken glass she had splintered against the rim of the swimming pool. I later left with my mother to be raised by her and dormitory proctors and my mother's lovers, one of whom had played football for the Colts. My father was scarred for life.

And now we were three—on the sofa, our feet on the rail. The night grew cool, Liz and Brian were happy for each other. I wondered when Liz would begin to change her style of dress and Brian would buy her a car.

"Goodnight," I said, wanting to sleep.

"Wait," Brian said. He followed me through the door, down the hall to the edge of the stairs.

I looked at him and smiled, put my arm around his shoulder the way we did at school, after a neighbor had made his girlfriend pregnant or performed marginally on an exam, and I said, "I'm happy for you, Brian. Really, I am." I thought of other things to say, but some things like marriages and timing, like glassware near a pool, seem just too fragile, and when a friend of yours like Brian makes a mistake, there's never any real need to tell him.

As for my parents, they were neither monogamous nor beautiful. I think at times there's no reason they ever should have been. I stopped at the medicine chest, the kitchen, the window over the street, removing my clothes as I went. All the rain was gone now, the street outside smelled clean and wet. I stood and listened to the building shift, to the wind rustle a drape. I listened to the pitch of Helen's breath coming from the bedroom.

Inside, she lay on her back, loosely wrapped in a twisted, spiraling sheet with her hand slipped below, the other to her ear now sliding to the rim of her navel. She opened her eyes and seemed to find direction, a sudden undercurrent of flux. Her hips began to swell in the light, rising slowly by degrees before falling equally slow to rise again while I stood by. In the light beneath the glow of the street, her shadow cast along the bedding, she grew buoyant, fluttering on the edge of flight. I watched her find her rhythm and watching her like that, so pleased with everything she could feel, so pleased with the very motion of herself, I felt as if we might never have to speak again.

BREATHING

IS KEY

Sarah, 1985

If I leave Eric, I'm not sure where I'll go. Maybe New Hampshire where I was raised. I have more things now than I used to, all these clothes I must have worn at one time or another. Downstairs, I hear Eric practice: small, bright points of music—harmonics, when he presses the strings lightly, not all the way down, but lightly so there's still space between. It's the air, he says, that makes everything ring.

He was playing at Fred's last May. The night was busy with people on their way to the canyon, and Eric had just arrived from a gig in Durango. When he asked for a beer, I asked for I.D. I asked him to play Neil Young, which he did. His voice is pretty and rough from smoking, from trying to sound rough, and you could tell he was working hard, stretching out the soft important parts because it was a request, because someone really wanted to listen to him. Later I told him he sang real nice.

"Actually," he said, "I play a lot better than I sing."

And I could feel it, the energy you feel when someone says something like that. It made me flush, the energy, filled me with nervousness and ideas, as if all those ideas were crawling up through my skin and climbing on top—like something from chemistry, when fire meets water and makes steam. It may look like a nice spring cloud, but you can tell from the smell it's going to be hot before it all goes away.

––––––––––

My mother died of stomach cancer. When she was a little girl, she drank gasoline and had to have her stomach pumped. Years later, after everyone else was gone, she died from this big clot growing inside her. When they did surgery, they saw how much was there—all that black stuff. The doctor said he had to sew her back up, there was so much, and since now that everything had been exposed to air she'd go fast. I said she had swallowed gas when she was young, could that have caused it?

"Probably not," he said, meaning it was just something that happened—the way this conversation happened, over the phone long distance.

This was the first important story I told Eric, one of those things which matters to you though you're not sure yet how it changed your life. Eric said he understood, that he had swallowed only a little, that he wasn't going to die from stomach cancer.

"It's not like I feel guilty or anything."

"It doesn't taste the way it smells," he said.

It made me wonder, though. What it tasted like. What cancer really tasted like. I never really knew my mother. She was just this woman who took care of me and told me to use protection, who bought me books for school and new dresses. She worked hard, fed my father, and when I left home I tried to say good-bye, but of course I didn't.

The Governor says I wouldn't be the same person if I had, or if I'd stayed, or if I'd done anything else in my life different than I have. He says this is what makes us what we are. Since Eric came to town, the Governor and I have gotten to know each other pretty well. Always before he was the thin guy who owned the gas station on Smith and didn't talk much. He has enough to say, though. He says if I need a loan to get to New Hampshire where I'm from I've got it.

––––––––––

Eric has stopped playing, I listen to him climb the stairs. He knocks because he knows I'm still upset. He knocks softly, opens the door a crack to see in.

"Sarah," he says, "are you hungry yet?"

"No," I say. "I'm cleaning."

He's also smoking a cigarette, which until yesterday he'd stopped doing. The smoke wanders in the room and curls up the doorway we painted together last fall. We painted it fire-engine red and built shelves inside the closet. His doctor told him if he didn't quit smoking he'd get emphysema. He said it was time to stop. Quit, he said. Quit smoking and save your life.

So Eric saved his life for about twenty days and in the process ruined mine. He was crabby. He ate fast food. He'd walk around the house and scream about the way the window wouldn't shut right, or the way the Governor never pumped any more gas now that he had his flunky, or the way I never wanted to do it anymore.

"What the hell happened to you?" he yelled. "I'm trying to do something here to make you happy and you can't even pretend!"

This was last night, after he started smoking again, before it happened. It's not as if he hadn't already had a cigarette. He'd been sneaking them all day behind the porch. He should have been calm, it shouldn't have happened.

"Do you like to pretend?" I screamed back. "Is that what you like to do?"

And then I saw his eyes, thinking about what that meant, which was more than I'd intended. They went blank for this time that was longer than it should have been—this blank empty space in his eyes, the hand swinging across the way things go before a crash, slow and fast at the same time because the speed doesn't really matter anymore.

It's something Michael used to do. It's something I was afraid made me feel different than I should—as if by deserving to be hit I was somehow hitting back at the same time, only harder because you couldn't really see it. And then I heard him say it, which is what they always say one way or another, "Oh, Jesus. Jesus, I'm sorry," as if they've forgotten already who I am and I'm not even sure I mind.

Next week after that first night at Fred's, I saw him at the Governor's. Besides owning the local Chevron, the Governor has been writing this phone book for twenty years. Each day he makes up a name, and he says it keeps him happy. He always has someone to call. At first Eric was just going to work for him until he paid off the parts for his engine. He seemed nice enough for a musician, too. If you fall for someone who travels around, you don't have to worry about being stuck. The way it had always been before, I got stuck, but Eric seemed mobile, not like the Governor, or even me sometimes, stuck between a rock and a hard place, which leaves no room at all for anything else except maybe yourself.

Eric came out and helped me put gas in the car. It was self-serve, so his coming out to help was supposed to mean something. It was one of those days when the sky is blue though you still know the rain is going to fall, for a little while, maybe after lunch. The dust smells sweet and ready to be rinsed. In New Mexico, the sun is hot and more powerful than most places. It will make you burn easy, the sun. I remember watching him fill my car, leaning with one hand on his hip, the other on the back of my dusty brown car. He could have written in it if he wanted, could have taken his finger and run it through the dust the way he does his guitar strings and said something. Instead, I told him he played real well. I asked him how long he'd be in town.

"For a while," he said, smiling. "I'm younger than you, aren't I?"

He was trying for another reaction, leaning against my car, filling it up with gas. You could see the vapors swimming in the air around the nozzle. They made the air look blue like the cool part in a fire.

"I don't know," I said.

"Do you mind?"

"Mind what?"

"Mind me asking?"

"No, Eric, I don't mind," I said, which tripped him up, my knowing his name. "You were born in 1960," I added, remembering his I.D. It surprised me that I'd remembered that, made me wonder why, which made me realize I must have wanted to.

The pump clicked shut. Eric tried to squirt more in, or maybe he was trying to pull it out and his finger hooked the trigger, because it came shooting out, spraying him with gas. He pulled the hose away, still shooting gas, and he couldn't get it to stop. This gas was shooting all over the Governor's driveway and spilling everywhere, and I saw Eric turn the nozzle, facing it to see what was wrong until he was really soaked. I heard him yell, drop the hose, his hands over his face, cussing, spitting—all in the same amount of time it took me to realize why I must have wanted to remember his I.D.

After the nozzle hit the cement, it shut off by itself. The Governor came out smoking a cigarette.

"There's gas all over!" I yelled.

I reached down to Eric, who was now kneeling by a hose, squirting water in his face. "My eyes," he kept saying. "My eyes!"

"Bring him inside, Sarah."

But Eric didn't want to go anywhere. I stood by and told him to let the water keep going, keep his eyes open, it would all wash out. When I finally helped him to his feet, led him into the garage, he felt cold and smelled like gas. We took him to the big sink and kept rinsing his eyes, which the Governor said would probably be okay. The Governor gave him a dry pair of pants, about nine sizes too long, and said Eric should really get his eyes checked. After he changed and was dry I drove him up to the clinic where this nice nurse in slacks asked if we were married. She irrigated Eric's eyes with special fluids. Later, I drove him back to his van, parked behind the Chevron, which seemed more lonely than I wanted to be.

And all that night, this is what I kept thinking. I kept thinking if there had been just one spark between us, one little match, the whole place would have exploded. It would have sparked and breathed in all the space around us until we were one big flame. Me, the Governor, Eric—in this flame turning our bones into hot white coals until, after, there would have been nothing left. Just ash in the shape of bones and the pink, dangerous smell of gasoline.

For the entire next week, Eric's hair smelled like gasoline.

We moved into a small two-bedroom. I cocktailed at Fred's and Eric played once or twice a month. We'd go swimming at the culvert, we'd have supper with the Governor. When Eric found out he had to quit smoking, he told us that night at the Governor's. He told us how he could still quit and have his lungs fix themselves, the damage wasn't total. He said it would help him breathe, especially here where the air is thin and higher up than normal.

"Breathing is key," said the Governor, nodding.

"Exactly," said Eric, lighting one up. "Which is exactly why I'm going to quit." He sat looking at the smoke, convincing himself.

We ate Mexican pasta in the Governor's kitchen. On the walls of his house are pictures of families he's gathered from local garage sales; he's given the pictures names and included them in his phone book. The Governor showed us his entry for the day—*Haverstock, Ed. 538 Maryland.* He still hadn't figured out the phone number, though he was sure of the prefix, and he said this name was particularly interesting.

"You don't know, you see, if Ed is short for Edward or Edith, and since whoever this Ed is lives over on Maryland with all the other middle-aged married people, we don't know yet how Ed is going to interact with his or her neighbors. Or with their children. We also don't know how Ed gets by."

Maryland, of course, was as made up as everything else, like the yellow pages and the number *538* which the Governor said would extend the street an extra block. He went on to speculate how the neighbors would react to a forty-year-old divorced woman or an aging mail clerk about to receive Social Security, or other types. We sat around his desk looking at his computer screen, with the name and address in orange square fuzzy type, wondering. Behind the desk on a wall was a map of his city drawn with big markers and names crossed out and rewritten and crossed out again. He saw me looking at the map, no longer listening, and pulled out a bottle of gin. We sat around his desk drinking gin while Eric smoked and I wondered how it was I had ended up here and not somewhere else. At 538 Maryland, or some other place. Once, I thought I wanted to live in California.

That night we walked home a little drunk. Eric kept his arm around my waist singing James Taylor and swaying to make me laugh. He was in a good mood because he hadn't yet decided when he was going to quit smoking, and it made me sad, his being in a good mood and singing while the Governor stayed up at his desk typing and retyping the names of people he didn't even know.

When we reached the house, Eric went inside and I went out to the porch, near the garbage cans and barbecue. I reached under and pulled out a half-empty gallon of gasoline. The can had rust growing along the top and the paint was faded red and splotchy. When I went inside, I poured us each a shot, but decided that was a little much. I emptied one glass, and put half the other inside because all I wanted to do was know how it tasted—gas, petroleum by-products. I wanted to know what it did to you inside.

Naturally, I didn't tell Eric. I just set his shot on the coffee table, near his feet, saying, "Hey, Cowboy, how 'bout a nightcap?"

I drank mine fast and wasn't surprised very much, though Eric was right: it doesn't taste the way it smells.

"To your not smoking," I said, which was the wrong thing to say. I should have said, "To your touring with The Dead," or "To your first album." Instead I said, "To your not smoking," and I think he figured it out because after I sat on the floor I could hear him calling the poison control center for instructions.

Once you reach your late twenties, you begin to know why you do things, though it doesn't always change you from doing them. On the edge of thirty, you see patterns, trends, maybe you start to understand what anyone who's ever been close to you already knows. Lately I think a lot about my mother, wonder what it must have meant for her to be thirty and married to my father, why it is I won't ever be married again. I wonder if she could explain it to me any better?

"Sarah," Eric says, "you can't keep doing this."

"Doing what?"

"This," he says, pointing at my clothes. They lie all over the floor and bed and dresser because I'm still trying to figure out what I want. He's stepped inside the room now, looking for a place to put his cigarette since all the ashtrays are put away. I had just gotten used to having my clothes smell like soap instead of smoke.

At first when it happened, it didn't really hurt. I just had this feeling that everything had stopped, including my breath. Still, so that nothing moved or beat, and then I did try to breathe, which meant I was just dizzy. And I remember thinking I used to like that feeling because it always meant something big was going to come up, or could come up, and then I remembered how I got that feeling.

"Eric," I say, watching him pace, "I want to go to the culvert."

Eric's van is one you could live in—big, long, a bed in back, a green cabinet with drawers, a cooler built into the wall. Inside, with the motor running, it sounds like a Volkswagen, and from the mirror hangs a tiny crystal an old lover must have given him because I can't imagine Eric ever buying it. I sit up front, my leg propped on the dash while Eric navigates the blind, twisting roads up to the culvert. He thinks the worst is over. I can tell by the way he sings with a tape, by the way he looks over sometimes when he thinks I'm not looking, which makes me think maybe it's not as big a deal as I'm making it into, or maybe I just want to make it into a big deal.

Either way, my cheek feels swollen and stiff. If I had this van, I could put most of my clothes inside the drawers in back. Right now, they're still scattered in the room, taking up the same amount of space they fill. Slips, sweaters, bras—without a person, they're just empty scoops of nothing. It's enough to make you wonder why buy them. Why take them with you? And if I don't go, it's no problem. I just put them all back on the shelves where they belong. I remember Eric, when he was playing at Fred's that very first night, under a hard light, a cigarette pinched between the strings at the top of his guitar, its smoke making the room cloudy and blue—the picture seems so still and permanent, and I think if memory is fixed, how come things change? How come I'm in this van and the elevation keeps climbing?

———————

Because this is where I am. This is why I'm here.

After it happened I spent the night at the Governor's. I walked to his place, stood outside watching the light in his office until I finally decided I didn't want to wait anymore. We sat at his round kitchen table. He made me tea and drank gin, and he said it was a hard thing to do, to stop smoking, but we both know that's not why Eric hit me. We both know he'd rather be some place else, same as anyone.

"What do you want, Sarah?" he said, knowing I didn't know what I wanted, that I just wanted things to be different and that I was really trying hard not to be bitter.

"He hit me," I said. "It's all starting all over again!"

Later, after I calmed down, the Governor put me to bed on his couch. He said if I still wanted the money he'd have it ready. My mother was bitter. The truth is, everyone I know *is*, except maybe the Governor, and he's just pathetic. I could hear him inside his room typing, sometimes thinking, followed by more typing on his keyboard covered with grease from the gas station. I could hear him talking to all those dead people on all those chips inside his orange computer.

———————

The second most important story I told Eric was that when I left Michael I didn't tell him where I was going. I didn't tell him I *was* going. I just left. I told Eric I still wasn't sure what it meant, and Eric made me promise to tell him first if I was ever going to leave. This was after I drank milk, sitting on the floor with a half ounce of gasoline in my stomach. The milk didn't help, I still had to vomit. I kept brushing my teeth, sitting on the floor with a pan of water to rinse the brush. I told him I felt sick but was glad now I knew what it tasted like.

Eric pulls the van up to a tree near the trail, where we always park under this tall, wide pine. The air smells like the tree, sharp and pretty. We climb out of the van and walk up the trail. Eric leads with the flashlight, though we don't really need it because the moon is almost full. It looks lopsided, it's so full.

We reach the top, walk across the bare, smooth stone. Under the ledge is Hadam Creek, forty feet straight down. Even in the dark you know the water is clear. Eric sets the flashlight on the stone, pointing up, and we take off our clothes.

I'm first to go: I look, breathe, leap. It takes longer than you think, and suddenly it's ice cold water in the dark and everything is numb. After, it feels like sex; I stand near the rocks and feel my knees shake. I wait, dizzy and light, and watch Eric sail through the black sky. I'm waiting where the water's knee-deep and when he finally comes over, sputtering, laughing, I look at him and try to make the picture stick, wondering if I can or what kind of name the Governor would most likely use for someone like me.

———————

We stand together near the top looking down. The water looks silver and almost bright, and if you look down at it long enough you can't tell really if you're looking down or up or even if it matters. Right now Eric's smoking a cigarette, pulling the red ash down into the filter, deep into his lungs. The hot ash makes his face glow, and his free hand rests on top of my shoulder as if we were best friends. He seems so relaxed now that we're friends. When he finishes the smoke, he'll want to jump together, and maybe under the water we'll wrestle together until we come up for air. I think this is something I'm going to remember for a long time, and that if I remember it, then things are going to change, because that's how it works. I can stay here and try to make things right, go to counseling, see what it is we need to make right. I think we have a lot here and not all of it's bad. I can forgive and make sure it doesn't happen again. I don't have to be bitter.

"Ready?" he says, flicking away the butt.

"Wait," I say, wanting to look. It's the anticipation that makes me wait; I know this now. Eric looks at me, smiling so his mouth curls just a little, and I think this time it's going to be different because I've made a promise: I'm going to have to tell him. I think it's something my mother would want me to do.

So I take his hand and jump.

THE McCLENAHAN

STROKE

Orion, 1976

Cass is younger, so I'm the better swimmer. Dad used to swim
in college, that's how he met Mom. He set a school record for the
two-hundred fly which wasn't broken until 1974. When someone called from his old college to tell him, he said to Mom,
"Well it's about time, by cracky."

We're in the lake swimming across at a lazy breaststroke. We
do this after practice every day mostly because there isn't much
else to do. Cass is only thirteen, but he's a strong swimmer, and
Dad says he'll be better than me, which is fine with me because
I only like to practice.

The trees around the lake are dark green, the water's wide in
this part and probably deep. On the beach somewhere is Little
Bingo, our English sheepdog. Dad named Bingo after a tank in

Korea, and Cass pulls slowly in front because I let him. His head floats and the top of his red hair is almost dry from the sun. The breeze is strong, but we're with the current now.

Cass has been pretty screwed up lately because last spring his best friend Peter Jowalski died and Cass saw the whole thing happen. Mom says this is why Cass gets so moody. She says I should be nice to him and not give him any grief. "Orion," she said, "Cass is having a bad time." We were in the kitchen, she was making pie, and Cass was outside sitting in the tree where the apples came from. When he was little he used to call it his tree fort, even though it was just a tree. Now he just calls it his tree—and that's why Mom's making pie, what she calls Cass Pie, in honor of Cass and his tree and because he's all screwed up since Peter Jowalski died.

"He needs to make more friends, Mom."

"Yes," she said, "but sometimes it's not easy to make new friends. You remember how it was when you first went to school?" She gave me one of those looks she gives you—with her eyebrows, mostly—when she knows she's right and doesn't want you to make her prove it.

"I hardly know anyone here anymore," I said.

"You have to let him know he's your friend," Mom said. "And be nice to Helen."

Helen swims for Lake Forest; she used to be my girlfriend. Before I left for prep school last fall, Helen said she didn't want to get real serious, and I said that was okay, so we're still friends. Helen is Peter's sister and Mr. Jowalski is one of Dad's partners in Chicago. They own a law firm called Jowalski, Blake, McClenahan and Ryan. You'd think Mom would have known she didn't have to tell me to be nice, but just right then I didn't feel like going into it.

Cass has started a crawl, free and side to side, so he knows where to go. His feet leave white bubbles in the green water from the way he kicks. I start a crawl too and keep up, breathing on every third stroke to save energy. Sometimes, if you float real still, you can feel the fish try and bite you, though we're going too fast for that now. We're probably scaring all the fish, and I want to tell Cass to slow down so he won't cramp up. Last summer we took Lifesaving together and learned all about cramps and how to keep drowning people from drowning you. My favorite is the nerve pinch in the underarm. Even Dad will let go if you pinch him there hard enough. When we were little, Dad used to go swimming with us. He'd put his hands under our arms and throw us up in the sky and make noises like he was a whale and we were the water. Sometimes he'd let us dive off his shoulders, but that was before we got too big and I went off to school. Next year, Cass is supposed to go to Berkshire, and we'll be able to visit on weekends, which Mom says will help him adjust.

Later, when the Jowalskis came over, we wore regular clothes. Mom made Cass put Bingo outside so he wouldn't jump on the company. Mr. Jowalski brought a bottle of wine and kissed Mom, Dad kissed Mrs. Jowalski, and Helen stared at me. Helen is very pretty: she has short dark hair like Dorothy Hamill, the skater, with big round eyes. Her voice is low and raspy and sounds sometimes like fingers on a chalkboard, the way it makes you tingle and your blood rush—like when you're driving fast over a dip and everything goes *swoosh* and you feel as if your nuts are in your chest or some place else they're not supposed to be. I have a picture of her in my wallet. On the back it says, *Love, Helen.*

"Mac," said Mr. Jowalski, "Orion here's almost as tall as you!"

"Almost," said Dad. He was fixing Scotch and waters and a Jameson rocks for himself.

I was shaking Mr. Jowalski's hand, saying, "Hello, Mr. Paunch," when Cass walked into the room. Mrs. Jowalski turned and walked across the carpet in high heels with her Scotch and water. You could see her heels sink into the carpet, and Cass just stood there. Then she hugged him. She put her arms around him and spilled some of her drink, and she held him there like he wanted to be held, which is something even Mom doesn't do anymore.

Mr. Jowalski said he was on a diet now, since he'd given up not smoking, and then he punched me in the ribs. Mom came into the room with her Diet-Rite and looked at Dad, who was fixing himself another Jameson's.

"Mary," she said, and Mrs. Jowalski turned to Mom. "Will you give me a hand?"

"Look," said Mr. Jowalski, sucking in his gut, "just look at that, Mr. Skin n' Bones!" but I wasn't paying attention. I was looking at Helen, who was trying not to look at Cass. She stood staring at the holes in the carpet made by her mother's shoes.

Dad coughed and lit a Benson & Hedges, Mr. Jowalski started to tell one about three insurance agents who flew to Kenya, and I asked Helen if she wanted to play a game of pool.

"You too, Cass," I said. "We'll play cutthroat."

We're at the other end of the lake, about a mile and a half since we started. Cass slows down because to touch bottom is to cheat, and we can feel the long seaweed twisting around our legs.

The wind's picked up and you can see most of the sailboats heading for shore. Cass doesn't sail because once he got the mast of Dad's Butterfly, the *Ergo*, stuck in the bottom of the lake where it's shallow. He'd overturned the *Ergo* because he wanted an excuse to get in the water. Once in, though, he couldn't right the boat. Dad swam out and shifted the hull. Cass probably could have done it himself if he'd weighed more, but Dad jumped on the centerboard and set the boat right with one try while I watched Cass swim in to shore. On top of the mast hung a hunk of seaweed, like a flag, and Cass swam in on a fly because he didn't want to cry in front of Dad. The butterfly takes the most energy.

Cass told me later Dad didn't yell at him because it wasn't anybody's fault the lake was shallow there, but Cass said it was still his fault because he'd tipped it on purpose.

"I never told you not to tip it," Dad said. "Let's not discuss it further," which is what he always says when he's right. Mom just looks at you with her eyebrows, and Dad says, "Let's not discuss it further," which was really supposed to make Cass feel better even though now he still won't take the boat out.

Cass makes a thumping splash with one of his feet, the water goes *thwunk* and high up into the air, and now he's ahead of me in a backstroke, spitting up water from his mouth like he's a fountain.

I do the same, go into a backstroke and look at the sky: the clouds are thick and full of color, and my skin that's out of the water feels cold and full of goose bumps. We're going against the current hard now. The sun goes under some clouds, gray and not very bright, and the air turns cold as water.

That night after dessert we went outside, Cass and Helen and me. The night was warm and we sat on top of the old stables blowing cigarette smoke at mosquitoes. The stables sit at the bottom of this hill and look up at the house through the trees. The house is mostly windows so you can see what's going on inside at night, even in the guest room where Mom was fixing up the bed for the Jowalskis. Cass and I had figured out a long time ago that at night you could see inside and they could see only themselves. But now we were sitting on the stables smoking cigarettes, swatting mosquitoes and listening to the trees. After a while Helen leaned back with her head on my lap and I put my hands on her shoulders. I felt the ridges of her bra, which I knew was white.

When Peter died, Cass was staying over at the Jowalskis' in Evanston. The Jowalskis live near an El stop. Sometimes we go there at night to watch the trains fly by and crush coins or smoke. Helen and I used to go there and make out, before I left for school last year, before she decided she didn't want to get serious.

What you do is crawl up the side of the underpass where these beams make a bridge for the train, and you crawl through and up the beams like you would a tree. Before you know it, you're on the tracks. And that's what Cass and Peter did the night he died, except they were drunk; the Jowalskis were out with our parents and the Blakes, and Helen was watching the house.

"They never came home," she said. She knew about the beer but didn't tell anyone. It was Cass who told, that night on the roof.

"We only drank six," he said. "That's all."

When Cass and Peter reached the tracks on top of the wooden bridge, they started to walk along the ties, and then Cass said Peter stopped walking. "He just stopped," Cass said. "And I said, What's wrong? And then he turned and stared at me. His face was all white and he didn't move . . ."

Cass stopped talking and I could feel Helen's pulse beating fast beneath my fingers. Cass sat there and kept staring at his tree, and then he started to talk again, almost a whisper.

"He wouldn't move. I said, What's wrong, Peter? and he wouldn't move. And then he said, Cass, I think I've been elec-trocuted, and then he fell backwards, like the movies—straight back. His eyes were still open, and he started making noises like he was snoring. Only he was dead."

Helen sat up and I put my hands in my lap.

"I put my face over the rail," Cass said, "the third rail that did it. I put my face over it and I could feel it, you know? I could feel the electricity going through the air. I could hear it buzzing, and Peter was dead."

Cass was crying now, and he rubbed his face with his fists as if he were trying to make something hurt so it would be okay that he was crying.

Helen said, "It's okay, Cass."

And the way she said that with my hands in my lap made me decide she was more important than me, or maybe stronger. I wasn't a part of any of this and I wanted to be so I could be like them, so I could tell Cass it's okay and have it really mean something instead of just trying to be his friend or wondering what it meant to be really serious.

I reached over to Helen while Cass said, "He was just dead," as if there was nothing that was ever going to change it again, and Helen tried to touch Cass, who pushed himself off the roof and landed on the grass below. Cass hit and rolled on the soft grass while Bingo ran over to see if he was all right. Bingo followed Cass up the hill, and Helen and I stayed on the roof: her crying now, and me wishing she wouldn't so things would be normal again. She sat there crying and I put my arm on her shoulder and worried she might take it the wrong way.

After a while she stopped crying. "Sometimes I just think about him," she said, her voice all raspy and wet. "That's all." And then she smiled and wiped her face against my shoulder.

"It's okay," I said.

When Mom came out in her bathrobe she asked what happened to Bingo.

"He went inside with Cass."

"Is anything wrong?" she asked. Mom has bright red hair like Cass, and you could see it glowing in the light from the house.

"Everything's fine," I said. "Why?"

"No reason," she said, passing up blankets and pillows. She told us to sleep tight.

Later Cass came back out with more cigarettes, saying Dad was loaded now and wanted to go sailing in the morning. We spent the night out there, the three of us curled up together on the roof because Cass didn't want to sleep inside and Helen didn't want to be alone. For a while we watched Mom inside the house. She went from room to room to turn the lights, and I thought about Cass, who has been sleeping on the roof since it first turned warm.

Before I went away to school I taught Cass how to jump from the roof. "It's how you learn to parachute," I said. "When you hit the ground, you have to bend your knees and roll." Bingo was our army dog: we would strap a 16-ounce bottle of Coke to his collar with electrical tape, in case we got hurt, and Cass would feed him Oreos for saving us.

The next day was the bicentennial, and Dad decided he and Mr. Jowalski should enter the sailboat race. The lake was crowded and I helped them rig the *Ergo*. The wind was strong and Dad said they'd have a good race. Mr. Jowalski had never sailed, which is why Dad wanted him to come along instead of me, and Mr. Jowalski kept saying things like "Are you sure she knows how to float, Mac?" Dad asked me to get the thermos— the blue one with orange juice and vodka, and after I brought it to them I swam out to the raft where Cass and Helen were watching.

Helen was laying on her stomach with the straps of her blue bikini untied. Normally she wears a Speedo, but that day she had on her bikini and you could see the white parts of her skin. When she leaned up to talk, you could see almost everything, and after a while she stopped leaning up to talk. Cass was sitting by himself, so I went over to the edge and watched the fish nibble at our toes. I talked to some other girls and watched the race, thirty or so boats all floating around with the wind, and Cass kept his hands folded in his lap.

"Cold water's good for that," I whispered, and he started laughing. No one else knew what we were laughing at, and it was the first time I'd seen Cass really laugh since I'd been home. We jumped in the water and I splashed Helen. She leaped at the cold water, showing everything, and tied up her swimsuit. She was about to dive in on top of us when she yelled, "Look!"

Out around the third buoy was Mr. Jowalski screaming. The boat was adrift, the sail fluttering and loose, Mr. Jowalski trying to balance himself and yelling for help. By the time Mr. Jowalski dove into the water, Cass was already on his way. I saw Steve the lifeguard starting up the powerboat, saw Mom on the beach next to Bingo holding her hands. I stayed out in the lake treading water, watching. I watched Mr. Jowalski heave Dad onto the side of the *Ergo* and pound on Dad's back. After a while Dad pushed him away, and you could tell his head was sore and he was angry.

Both Cass and the lifeguard reached the boat too late to do any good. Dad had already taken the tiller and set about finishing the race. Mr. Jowalski held the sheet and looked confused while the wind played with the blue and pink sail.

Helen slid into the lake and swam over to where I was treading water.

"Is he okay?" she said.

"Sure. He just got smacked by the boom."

"What's the boom?"

"The big metal thing the sail sits on. When the wind shifts or you come about, you have to duck."

Helen smiled and said, "It looks like he's okay."

"Yeah," I said, "he's okay," but I was thinking about what Dad would say later that night. He'd say, "Let's not discuss it further," and what made me mad was that I knew no one would.

I knew Cass wouldn't win his race today because he'd already swam half the lake for nothing. I knew if the Fourth had been called off for rain, none of this would have ever happened, and then I tried to imagine how things would have been if Cass had died instead of Peter.

"I'm sorry," I said. I was sorry I was glad it was Peter who had been electrocuted and not Cass.

"What?"

"I'm sorry your brother died."

She looked at the water and watched Cass swimming towards us. Behind him, you could see Dad and Mr. Jowalski tack in the wind.

We're treading now, resting, and it looks like rain. The sky is black and thick, the wind stronger than it was. It's still not ready to rain, though. We have the eye to go through first. The eye is the quiet part before the rain comes, when you're surrounded by the storm but still not in it. The storm keeps swirling until it finally closes in and blows up the center. Then it turns into clouds and pulls itself back together again.

Since we're still in the eye, we don't have to worry much, though Cass and I are the only ones in the lake. There are no boats. No one's on the raft. It's just us, swimming the lake like we always do and me hoping we make it back before it starts lightning.

"Pick it up," I say.

"What?"

"We need to pick it up. It's going to storm!"

"Fly," Cass yells.

"What?"

"Fly! We can swim half the lake on the fly in the middle of a hurricane!"

And he takes off. His brown shoulders stretch and his arms

sweep the water, his legs swinging up and driving the splash into my face, and I think the lake smells pretty weird when you think about it. There's so much shit in it, really.

Dad and Mr. Jowalski came in second to last, and Cass didn't place at all against the parents: he said he wasn't into it. But I was. I took first in the fifty and hundred free, which wasn't unusual because I'm still the fastest on the team, even faster than the parents I swam against.

I also swam the free for the two-hundred medley, Dad did the butterfly and Cass the breaststroke. Mom did backstroke, and our family won. We might have lost because of Mom—she doesn't really swim that well—but Dad established our lead. I stood on the pier watching him with his sore head and bad lungs, only you couldn't tell his head was sore or his lungs hurt while he swam. You could only see his long arms working like wings while he kept pulling ahead and ahead, and Mom yelling, "Go, McClenahan! That's what I love! That's the McClenahan stroke! Go go go!"

We won more ribbons to put on the wall by the pool table; the Jowalskis said congratulations and Helen and I took Bingo for a swim. We made him fetch a tennis ball.

"Helen," I said, after we'd thrown the ball a while, "how come you just wanted to be friends?"

"What?"

"How come last summer you said you just wanted to be friends?"

She snatched the ball off the water and squeezed it between her palms, thinking. I could feel everything getting cold while I stood there in the water, not moving. I stood there waiting for her to say something.

"Because," she said finally, "I wanted us to stay friends."

She took the ball and snapped it with her wrist. The ball hit me on the forehead and she said, "Hey, Orion. Are you still my friend?"

I splashed her and gave her a good dunk—longer than I should have, and when we went back to the beach I pinned my blue ribbon on Bingo's collar and told everyone he'd earned it for swimming the English Channel last winter.

"Yeah," said Helen, "he was looking for sheep."

"That's 'cause he's a sheepdog," said Cass, and we watched him get up off his towel and walk away. Bingo sat on his towel, and Mr. Jowalski started to say something at the same time Dad said he was about ready for another.

"Helen," said Mrs. Jowalski, "tell the McClenahans about your trip to Washington."

———

Ahead of us is the beach, and Mom's standing on it with Bingo. She's waving at us with our towels to go faster, though we can't go any faster. The waves are thick and choppy and you can see lightning in the distance. I feel Cass beside me and our pace is together. And I'm pretending I'm Dad, in a college pool with lots of chlorine and about to set another record. The crowd is screaming, screaming so loud I can hear it under the water and I hear Cass beside me, my coach, pacing the deck yelling *Stroke! Stroke! Stroke!* and that's what I'm doing, flying with my arms in the water and aiming for Helen who's waiting at the other end. After a while my arms don't ache anymore, they're just doing what they should, and I can't even tell I'm breathing. I'm just doing it.

———

We watched fireworks that night, down at the lake, after the Jowalskis left. They had their own fireworks show in Evanston, and Mrs. Jowalski felt sick. When I said good-bye to Helen, she said she was glad we were still friends, and then she kissed me the way friends kiss.

Cass and I sat with Mom and Dad watching the fireworks go off into the sky, blowing up, and sometimes they'd still be lit when they hit the water and you could hear them sizzle.

"There goes another," Mom would say at the green ones, until all the green ones were gone and there was only the finale left. It went up and burst like thunder and the sky lit up with blue and green and white—stars exploding into bigger stars and all the people at the lake going *Oooh!* and *Ahhh!*

And then it was done, the fireworks were gone. We sat on the beach and Mom asked Dad how his head felt.

I didn't hear what he said because I wasn't listening anymore. I was thinking about Helen and wondering why she didn't want to be more than friends. I was thinking about the way when we climbed up the tracks and watched the trains she used to kiss.

It's raining now, cold water streaking the air and drilling the lake. Mom's still on the beach, waiting for us, yelling at us to hurry. There's thunder now and we're running out of the water up the beach. Cass trips once and I help pick him up. Bingo runs out and tries to jump on us but misses.

"Where have you been?" Mom yells.

"In the lake," I say.

"I can see that," she says, throwing us the towels. They're wet but still better than nothing. "Come on!" she yells, and runs up to the Datsun Dad bought after the gas crisis.

Inside, Bingo breathes hard and makes the car smell. I'm in the front with Mom, and Cass sits in the back and tries to make Bingo dry with his towel. The rain pounds down on the roof and everything's loud. Mom starts the engine and turns on the defroster, which makes things louder, and the windows still fog up. All you can see is the rain from the place the wipers make in the windshield.

"You could have gotten yourselves killed!"

"We couldn't help it, Mom. It was nice when we started."

And then she starts crying. "Damnit, Orion, you know better," and now she's crying hard. Her face turns red like her hair, and she starts pounding the steering wheel, screaming "Damnit! Damnit all!" and she keeps crying.

"Mom," says Cass. "It's no big deal. Nothing happened."

I give her my towel to wipe her face, and she tries to make herself stop. "I'm sorry," she says, "It's just—" but she's confused and tries to wipe the fog away from her window, and I know it's something bad. I can tell it's something bad by the way something's going on inside like when you're driving over dips, only worse, by the way I feel like I'm back inside the lake with the sky turning black in the center, watching for things to happen and trying to get out before they do.

———

Mom's on the phone now, in the kitchen talking to doctors from Chicago, and I feel like I'm still in the water, only I'm not going through it. It's going through me. I feel wet and cold, and I know I feel this way for a reason. We listen for a while, watch Mom concentrate, sometimes talking slowly. She waves us away, wipes her face with the back of her hand. She rubs at her cheek with the rings on her hand. The rings leave marks in her skin, and Cass and I go downstairs to the laundry room where the room smells clean like soap and apples. Mom has stacked fresh clothes on top the dryer.

"Dad's sick," Cass says, taking off his suit. "He has an aneurysm."

I walk over to the big sink to rinse my suit and wash the lake out of my hair. The water feels hot, runs over my shoulders down my spine, and I think that after Peter Jowalski died, straight back on the rails and drunk the way he wasn't supposed to be, Cass had to figure out what to do next. He had to figure out where to go, what to say. Most of all, he had to figure out why, but I don't care why. I just want to tell someone everything's going to be okay. I want to tell someone it's going to be fine like fireworks on the Fourth when the sky's lit up and your girlfriend puts your head in her lap and watches your face more than the sky.

"No," I say, practicing. "Everything's really going to be okay."

THE ANONYMITY

OF FLIGHT

Helen, 1990

I was living in Pittsburgh when Peter called from Vermont asking if wasn't it about time we "connected, saw how things worked." His voice lacked the same tenor I had come to associate with our conversations; it sounded empty and sad and hopeful, all at once. After I made the arrangements at work, I told Walt I needed some time away. At first he was displeased, standing in the kitchen drinking cranberry juice and studying my eyes.

"It's only a few days," I said.

"I know."

"It will do me good to see the country."

He shrugged, his shoulders thin in the dim evening light. Outside were noises from the city, a bus was gearing up, or down, and I paid more attention to its noise, thinking about the possible thickness of its exhaust, than to whatever Walt was about to say.

The morning I left, Walt drove me to the airport through an unexpectedly heavy snowstorm. Cars moved so slowly they slid off the incline of oncoming ramps; wipers beat furiously at the snow, people honked, everybody was late. The streets for a while had turned white, covered with thick moist snow, and I caught myself wondering how long it would last—this white, pretty snow in a city in Pennsylvania known for its dying heavy industries.

At the curb Walt kissed me good-bye, briefly, while I stood reaching for my bag, trying not to appear rushed.

"I'll call from Hartford," I said.

"Tell Peter hello," Walt said, which surprised me. I could feel the snow falling on my hair.

"It's just a visit," I said. "It doesn't mean anything."

A cop yelled, Walt smiled and said, "Have a good trip, Helen," and I watched him climb into his car. I wanted to wait, wanted to watch him drive off through the weather and noise. Through the car window I could see him adjusting a knob, and then he put the car in gear and drove away.

On the plane I sat near a man who drank Bloody Marys. I read through the airline magazine twice. I avoided his conversation. There is something faintly repellant about airline conversation, when you talk with someone you know you're never going to or probably never want to see again, especially men who by their very posture you can tell are feeling safe in the anonymity of flight. I read a long advertisement on the power of hypernatural vitamins and thought about Peter, whom I had not seen for seven, maybe eight months. Since New York, where Walt had business. I'd gone along thinking maybe I should. While Walt went to meetings, I visited the city and saw Peter on a street outside a theater. He was standing still, watching me carefully, cautiously, the dead eye patched, the other focusing hard, he'd said, because you were never supposed to see someone you actually knew in the city. I told him I was with Walt, we went and had coffee, we talked about Peter, old times. It took me a while to catch my breath.

We found a booth at a restaurant with vinyl seats, and he told me about his current situation where he served as care-taker of a "modest estate." Peter was always finding mentors. He went from place to place and let people with money fall in love with him. "But it's different now," he said. "I want to find a new place and dig roots. I want to settle for a while," which, I thought, meant he wanted to know now, here at this restaurant in New York City with me increasingly late for my meeting with Walt—I felt as if Peter wanted to know something more than I might possibly be able to give him. I receded. I told him about things that didn't matter, and when the waitress came by, an old, graying woman with heavy makeup, Peter let me take the check. "Thanks," he said, rising, "but I've really got to go," and I kept thinking about what that meant: his having to go while he walked away, his gait fast and loose, cutting between angry pedestrians and stalled cars, all those unfriendly people with all their lives while he walked away between them. I thought about roots and how deep and inextricable ours had always seemed. I wondered if maybe I was wrong.

Now I was on a plane trying to figure it out all over again, and the stop in Newark turned into a three-hour delay. All of New England was snowed in, including Hartford, which finally opened up long enough for us to land. The flight came in shaky, bumpy, the weather outside fast and white. Just as I was thinking we were safe, the hot melting scent of de-icing fluid still burning off the engines, the plane pitched in the wind. A sudden, desper-ate sweep while the passengers rushed into a scream, a swell of panic, the man next to me clutching my arm. We skidded on the runway and the jets went backwards, inside themselves and vio-lent, a loud white noise trying to slow us in the freezing wind. Finally we slowed to a taxi, the attendants began gathering small bottles of whiskey from a sprung cabinet, and the man removed his hand, smiling, trying to apologize but probably thinking that it didn't matter. We were safe, we were on the ground.

The captain's voice came over the loudspeaker, explaining in the aftermath that we had experienced a minor wind sheer, nothing unusual, and that now we were perfectly safe.

"For now," said a steward. "Sure, now that we're on the ground!"

I was still shaking when I left the plane, walking outside over the ice and into the terminal, thinking about all those planes which crash each year and kill everybody inside them, when I saw Peter. He stood behind a railing and angry passengers. Dressed in heavy wool, his face bearded, he seemed more easily prepared for the climate, and when he finally hugged me, put his arm around me and asked how I, the City Gal in Pumps, was doing, I decided to try and not think about it because maybe now was a time when it might not really matter.

"Fine," I said, watching his smile, my legs nervous, my voice unsteady and weak. "You look really good."

I woke the next morning in a strange, large room. The room smelled like cedar, the light came in from the east, making the room yellow and bright. I lay in a wide bed high off the floor with thick cotton quilts, and I realized I was in Vermont. I heard a voice singing, low in pitch and happy, and I could smell breakfast. Peter was cooking.

I put on a robe that hung from a door and wandered outside. Throughout the house, I recognized Peter's presence, though it was a new presence: large, dysfunctional ceramic bowls, a mobile in the dining room, pieces which he explained to me later he had given to the owner of this house—a Ms. Wilmington-Roch, Beth, who lived here alone now that her children were gone.

Later, after we spent the morning outside hiking through the snow, I asked Peter whose bed it was I had been sleeping in. We sat on the couch, our feet crossed, watching the fire.

"Beth's," he said. "I told you, she's away."

"Are you lovers?"

"That's an awfully personal question," he said, laughing, and I didn't press the issue, didn't want to make him feel compelled to tell, which made me wonder why I was here in this woman's house in Vermont anyway. I thought about Walt and wondered if he'd ever been to Vermont. In the spring, Walt wanted to see Jamaica, said if I wanted I was free to come along. That he would like that.

"Peter," I said, "what's up?"

He sat smiling, looking at me, knowing exactly how to gauge each phrase, and I looked at him a long time the way he would look at me, his eye tight in a squint and full of assessment. For Peter, time and space was all a matter of what he could touch.

"It's a matter of steps," I said, rising. "One follows the other." I kissed him. I said, "I'm going to take a nap, Peter."

My brother's name was Peter, a coincidence that has always troubled me—a sign that either Peter was in fact the right or the wrong person for my life. My brother died when he was thirteen. He looked nothing like Peter and, had he lived long enough to know him, probably would have found this older version entirely unlike himself. I never felt especially close to my brother until he died, and then he became inescapable. He followed me as I grew up, growing up right along with me, responding to my life now that his own was over—becoming what I thought he would want until I met Peter and tried finally to make him leave. Now I was thinking about going to Jamaica with a man named Walt, and I thought later that afternoon that we spend our lives looking for signs—for thin, brief moments of direction. And it was glorious, for a while, when Peter came into this strange woman's room, the space teeming between us with suddenness and nostalgia. The two of us on an unfamiliar bed where I knew only my lover. Until afterwards, after we lay back on fine, feathered pillows, breathing, steeped in relief and me thinking that the stars, even when they are out, hardly know who we are. That it is we who name them.

That next morning, Wednesday, Peter took me skiing. The morning was bright and clear. We drove through a strikingly deep landscape—so removed and distant from the black streets of Pittsburgh—here, where everything was layered with snow which would linger into May. He was taking us back, too, back to Boulder where all we did was ski. In the Rockies I had grown comfortable with the terrain, but here with trees and thin, empty roads in the depths of New England, I felt displaced and foreign. It was Peter who had taught me to ski well.

"It's different here," he said. "Less powder, more ice. It's faster too, sometimes. You'll like it."

He drove slowly with one wrist loose upon the wheel of Beth's Subaru station wagon; part of the deal, he explained, along with utilities. And I couldn't help wondering about Beth. I imagined her tall, maybe busty, with thin, fine hair. I wondered if he took her skiing. If perhaps they'd met while skiing. If she knew as much about me as I did her.

The slopes were fresh and clean, near empty. Peter adjusted my bindings, which belonged to Beth, along with the bibs; he reached down with a pocket screwdriver, turning, adjusting, telling me when to shift my weight. He was wearing sunglasses, concealing the patch and making him appear fully sighted. Watching him adjust my bindings—Beth's bindings—I remembered things I didn't want to.

We skied most of the day, him following me so I could set the pace. Towards noon, the mountain took on more people, mostly strangers from New York and Boston with voices as ugly as Pittsburgh's. Once, while standing in line waiting for the bottom lift, I watched a young boy—nine, maybe ten—all goggles and bibs. He was holding up the lift, apparently frightened by the prospect of riding alone. I slid up ahead, nodding to the attendant, and took my place beside the boy. I asked him if it would be okay if he gave me a hand.

"Uh huh," he nodded, feeling it out. We waited, plucked the next chair beneath us, and began our ascent. The chair rocked slowly while we balanced our weight. Twenty feet farther, all was silent, and we rose into the mountain.

"This is my favorite part," said the boy, watching the snow, the people sliding down below us.

"Mine too," I said. "Where's your Mom and Dad?"

"In Chicago."

"Chicago? I'm from Chicago!"

"Yeah, uh huh. I live on Wacker. My Dad's really smart, too. I go to a special school."

"In Vermont?"

"We ski every week. This is my fifth time," he said, holding up his hand. "The whole school skis."

"My name is Helen," I said. I reached to shake the boy's mitten, but he just looked at my hand, wrapped in Gortex, and then my face, wind-burned and cold. The air was turning colder with each passing pillar. I ruffled the top of his hat and asked if he was getting ready for the Olympics.

"Oh, yeah," he said. And later, "It's cold." The wind blew at us, we passed a sign preparing us to depart. "Get ready!" he said, his hands braced on top of the safety bar. When we passed the next sign, he pulled the bar over our heads. He clutched the arm of the chair and my thigh.

I saw at the edge of the next run a group of boys waiting. When we reached the lip of our exit, I slid on ahead, hoping he wouldn't fall in front of his friends. He passed behind me and turned, pushing hard reaching for balance and speed, yelling "So long, Helen!" and waving with one of his poles. After he skidded into his friends, I watched them turn, pivot, searching for the right slope. When they were gone, I was still waiting beneath the lift, waiting for Peter—what we'd always done even when he was waiting for me. I decided to go on ahead.

I couldn't help it, I could not escape us. I measured my life with an uncertain calendar. I'd compare my career to his. My life with our past. When he asked for money, I'd sent it. When he called me up, I'd follow. I'd upset my life and go to Vermont and talk with a man whose clothes I didn't even recognize while I tried to keep everything good about us close. I was by myself, thinking about Jamaica and why it was Peter who had wanted to connect. He was still waiting for me to take the lead, the way he followed me down the runs, or the way he pushed me to leave him in the first place, or the way I let him push.

My father once told me to button my blouse. I was going out on a date with a boy, the son of one of his partners, and he looked at me across the foyer, cigarette in hand, and while I stood reaching for the door he said, "Helen, button up your shirt. You look like a tramp!"

If my mother had said this, it would have been different. But my mother was shaky, and my brother's death had upset her balance: she grew more efficient, more evenly detached. And my mother didn't say this, my father did, the man who looked like my brother, only older, and later, after he died, I went to my father. I went to him and explained what had happened and my father cried. He put his arms around me and wept. He told me he loved me. That never would anything bad happen to me ever. Later I came to realize he wasn't sure who I was exactly. And maybe himself, who he was, the famous Chicago lawyer who lost his son in a freak accident. If Peter hadn't died, I think things surely would have been different, and if there is a reaction for every action, a meaning for every moment, then maybe this was it—this difference he made everything have.

"I don't buy it," Peter said. It was morning, we lay on a couch drinking juice, watching the sun. My muscles ached. My bones felt healthy and tired.

"All action is random," he said, "it derives meaning from its randomness. It means because it happens."

It made me happy, talking this way in our old, familiar language. "I hope that made sense to you," I said.

"Perfect. It's all connected. Threads of an intricate, unpredictable web. Think about your brother, Helen. Do you think he thought his life was meaningless? No. The only one who ever worries he ever got any meaning is you, and that's just because you're worried about your own."

"What about you? How come you have only one eye?"

"Why do birds fly?" he said.

"Why do airplanes fly—tell me that."

He sat up, stretched, his long arms popping in their joints. "I don't know," he said, yawning. And later, after I'd fallen asleep, I woke with him somewhere nearby, and I remember hearing him say something.

Sometimes I wish I could remember what it was he said. Maybe I should have listened more closely. Maybe it would have changed things even more. Either way, I grew up believing we each had a star. After the accident, I named the North Star after my brother because I thought that might be his and because it was the only star in the sky I could locate consistently. I remember thinking even then the act hopeful and larger than myself. In Vermont, watching the cold, night sky, black in a realm of small, pointed lights, I thought of all those stars floating above us, spinning and burning, and all of that black space which separated each. I thought it no wonder we invented constellations. Because we needed something to keep our stories straight.

My mother and father met at Vanderbilt, dated, quarreled, made up and quarreled some more. My father left for law at Trinity; my mother, an art department in Detroit—she drew pictures of Chevrolets while my father studied torts. Later they met in Chicago quite by accident. They went to a restaurant, drank coffee; they married and had children, and I couldn't help thinking the same would always happen to me when I was ready. That despite our past, when Peter and I met in New York we were somehow embarking on a new course of mutual destiny.

In the meantime, Peter worked in his studio—a renovated woodshed that he wouldn't let me visit. The night I decided to leave, we skied medium slopes offering lights. I had never skied at night before, racing completely alone watching my shadow skimming over the hard, frozen snow. My edges were dull, I slipped more than I liked, but I was still by myself with Peter always nearby. It made me feel safe, skiing in the dark with him so close behind. It made me not mind the ice that I could never clearly see. Later we drank beer in a lodge with other locals. We sat on the bench of a picnic table, backwards, with our feet stretched out and our backs to the table drinking cold, dark beer.

"You know," he said, "with a few more days, you'd be as strong as ever."

When we drove home that night, the toes of our skis hanging overhead like smooth, frozen feet, I knew I wasn't going to fly again—not after the incident at Bradley. The skies were too crowded, the weather unpredictable. I sat in the car and let Peter drive and decided to tell him I was going to rent a car from Hartford.

"Jesus," he said. "That's a long trip."

We were walking now, together up the long, private road which led to the house. The weather was shifting, the snow unevenly white. We walked slowly under the sky, our hands deep in our pockets, our arms looped at the elbows.

"I'll have to leave early."

"You know," he said, slowing to turn and face me, "I like it here." He removed a hand, let it sweep the frozen property. "I like this place. The Green Mountain State."

"It'll be a long drive."

He nodded, we resumed our walk towards the house. The weather was too cold to linger in even with someone you knew. At the top of the drive, I watched the house glow with unfamiliar lights.

"Beth," Peter said. "She's back."

I tried to detect a change in voice, a flutter of anxiety, but there was none. We walked straight to the door, swung it open, Peter calling, "Beth!" and me following along after wiping my feet.

She was standing in the kitchen leafing through her mail. Tall, slender, with cropped graying hair and reading glasses, she was my mother's age and made me for a moment feel odd.

She and Peter exchanged hugs, kissing each other's cheek; I watched Peter and the ease with which he did this.

"Hello!" she said to me brightly. She reached out her hand, taking mine.

"I'm Helen," I said.

"Yes, yes. I know." She looked to Peter, then me. "Come," she said, looking me over, smiling.

I followed her into the big room while Peter fixed a fire. Beth had removed her shoes, her toes curling beneath her tights. She wore a long heavy skirt and sweater. This morning, she explained, she'd been in Seattle.

And we talked easily, she and I, which later made perfect sense—for me to be comfortable with someone Peter too was comfortable with. We laughed often, and eventually I stopped feeling as if I were being interviewed. I told Beth I would be leaving in the morning.

"Not on my account, I hope."

"No," I said. "Not at all."

"It's lonely here, you know. It's lovely, sure. But it's lonely. You live in the heart of some place lovely, but it's just you and who you know." She smiled briefly, gestured toward Peter. "It's not like the city, which can be ugly and lonely. It's a more profound loneliness somehow when everything is beautiful and perfect. The way I suppose Greece would be, or Jamaica."

"Jamaica?"

"Well, I suppose Jamaica's growing more and more crowded now, isn't it? Maybe Brazil."

"It's lovely," I said. "I never pictured it this way."

"Could you stay for one more day? I'd love to show you what Peter missed. He's so focused, sometimes he misses things."

"No," I said. "I really can't."

"Well you must come back then. That's all there is to it!" She rose, her skirt fell evenly in place. She'd see us in the morning. "Which room are you staying in?" she asked.

I looked at her, at Peter; I was unsure where I was supposed to be.

"Fine," she said, smiling. "I'll take the boys' room," and she left, saying goodnight once again before ascending the stairs with her mail and a cup of tea.

"That's Beth," Peter said.

"She's wonderful. She's really wonderful."

He shrugged, sipped at his drink. "Let me show you something," he said, rising.

I followed him, slipped on a pair of Beth's boots and a large, musty sweater. We walked out back through the snow toward his studio. Inside, the room smelled like clay and the lingering scent of woodsmoke. It felt cold and empty. He flipped a light—a bare bulb which hung from a beam by an electrical cord—and along the wall, surrounding his wheel and tubs of clay, were photographs he had taken of me when we were together: all of them nudes. *A Study of Helen.* The prints were tacked to the wooden walls with small, rusty nails, and the weather had caused some of the prints to warp.

"I should have been more serious," he said. "They're easier to put in books."

For a brief moment I wasn't sure of place, or time, as if suddenly I had been sent back through four oddly consecutive years of my life, back through my time alone or with others until Peter. The room grew strangely familiar, I recognized the smell of clay, the cold dryness of the air and the weight of my sweater.

"It's not how I am anymore," I said.

"What do you mean?"

"It's not how I am. It's not how you are. Those," I said, pointing, "those don't change. Don't you see? Don't you see that? We're not the same anymore. Jesus, Peter, I'm not twenty-three with a boyfriend from college. I'm not some thing from a myth!"

"You don't think so?" he said, laughing. "Then how do you explain it?"

He meant the pots and sculptures in the room, all the pieces he hadn't sold or given away. He meant all the clay waiting to be shaped. I reached for the photos and began pulling them down, one by one, each of them, leaving bits of paper beneath the nails while I pulled them off the wall and tore them to shreds. I tore them into small pieces and let them float to the floor and wondered how many people I didn't know had seen me in this room while Peter thought about what he was going to do with me next. Later I apologized because I knew I had destroyed something that wasn't wholly mine. And it felt awful, that sense of guilt and selfishness and absolute uncertainty. It made me feel empty inside. Hollow.

In 1986, in Boulder, Colorado, I became pregnant; the fetus aborted itself of its own free will—a black, pithy symbol. All while I was pregnant, I had thought maybe we could name the boy, if it was a boy, Peter. We could make a boy and give my brother another chance which I owed him because he did not have to die at the age of thirteen. So, I thought, maybe this was more than accident. Maybe we really were participating in the making of a sensible, meaningful world. Which is what mattered, the making of something meaningful. Peter had his pots. The baby died.

In the morning I said good-bye to Beth. She took me in her arms, told me to come back, and she made me feel warm and strange, this woman who knew only what I looked like. She made me feel shy and angry with Peter all over again.

After a long, silent drive through Massachusetts into Hartford, Peter said, "Look, it was a fluke. It would be a lot easier just to fly."

"No," I said. "Besides, I want to drive. It will give me time to be by myself."

I rented a large Ford while Peter bought me a map. "Follow 91 to 284," he said, "and follow the signs to 80." The map lay spread on the hood of the car. I watched his finger following the small, colored lines of the map. Overhead I could hear the sound of airplanes, and when I kissed him good-bye, I stood in front of the car not wanting to say anything large.

"It was a good visit," I said.

And I drove away. I drove away through Connecticut, part of New York, and into Pennsylvania. Pennsylvania is a long state, and I was driving late into the night when I decided to look for a motel. I was tired of driving, of being by myself. I was in a car on a dark road driving faster than I should when I saw the brief shadow of something move, the bright glare of a strange animal's eye—yellow, still, a round heavy marble. The car jolted with a sudden thud, something heavy hit the roof, and I skidded off the road towards a ditch, perfectly calm, thinking *This is it. This is it.* Inside, the air grew cold and I felt myself shaking all over again. I left the car and saw behind me the shape of a horse, a young horse the size of a deer. A filly or colt. She lay very still bleeding on the pavement.

I felt the wind, the cars passing me by on the highway. I thought I should try and move her but I knew I couldn't. Instead I stood by and watched a truck come by and hit her again, dragging her beneath the frame of the truck while I stood by on the side of the road. I turned and went to my car and sat in it very still, thinking about the man on the plane in Hartford, clutching my arm while we almost crashed—how grateful I was now to have had that hand, that strange man's hand grabbing my arm now that it was over. I thought about what I would tell Peter later, in a letter, that it didn't matter if you flew or not if you weren't more careful. Up through the windshield I could see the stars burning over Pennsylvania. In Pittsburgh you couldn't see the stars, the lights from the city were simply too bright, and I wondered if maybe this wasn't such a bad thing. I wondered if all this meant something I was going to understand but didn't want to.